D.A.W.G. TALES

DOWN ASS WHITE GIRLS
volume one

D. King/Q. Grover

D.A.W.G. TALES

A Penny Publication

A QUICK NOTE TO THE READER:

THE STORIES IN THIS BOOK ARE MEANT TO BE
USED FOR ENTERTAINMENT PURPOSES ONLY,
AND THE SCENARIOS ARE NOT INTENDED TO
OFFEND, DEGRADE, 0R BELITTLE WOMEN OF
EUROPEAN DESCENT IN ANY FORM.

ANY SIMILAR SITUATIONS, PLACES, NAMES, OR
OTHERWISE, ARE NOT INTENDED TO
RESEMBLE ANY PERSONS ALIVE, OR THAT
HAVE LIVED, AND IF THEY DO, IT IS PURELY BY
COINCIDENCE.

OUR HOPE IS THAT THIS BODY OF WORK IS AS
ENTERTAINING TO ITS READERS AS IT WAS FOR
THE AUTHORS.

D.A.W.G. TALES

Down Ass White Girls

volume one

OH MY FUCKING GOD, AMANDA!!

"Oh my fucking God, Amanda!! This is the third different nigger I've seen dropping you off at this house this week, and at this time of night!! The first time I caught your ass, you said he was just a friend from school. The second one you claimed that he was the school's star point guard and that you were his tutor. So who's the third one, Barack Obama's fucking nephew?!" Amanda's father John yelled at her as she walked through the front door.

"Dad I really wish you wouldn't be such a fucking racist all the time!! You make yourself sound so damn ignorant. Geez, u should grow up." Amanda replied back. She hated the things he'd said to her and how he behaved about her having black friends.

"What, you have a problem with me using the word *nigger*?" Hell, I don't see anything wrong with it, and apparently they don't either, as much as I hear that word come outta their mouths!!" he continued.

"Dad your just plain out wrong for the way you treat me. I'm a straight A student, I don't do drugs and I'm never into any trouble, yet all you do is nag and ride my ass since mom left you. And I'm starting to see why dad, and it's because you are an asshole, and I fucking hate u!" she said and stormed off to her room and slammed the door.

Once inside she dialed her mother's new house phone number, needing to hear her voice. Her mother always made her feel better after she'd had a bad day. Her mother's name was Amy and she had a light and bubbly personality. Her energy and attitude were high since she'd left John for a black man that everyone referred to as Silk, because he was so smooth with the ladies.

"Hey lil momma, what'cha up to today?" Silk's voice said into the receiver, answering the phone. He was always nice to Amanda.

"Oh. Hi Silk, Is my mom there?" she asked trying to conceal crying into the phone.

"No, sweetheart, she just stepped out, but she'll be right back. Is everything alright baby girl?" he asked, genuinely concerned.

"Yea I'm fine, I just need to talk with my mom right now," she replied, now audibly breaking down on the phone.

"Awe what's the matter baby girl? You can talk to me about it until Amy gets back if you want," he offered, trying to console her.

"Well for starters, my dad's being a real fucking dick to me for absolutely no reason, and he's saying really mean stuff to me and I don't deserve to be treated like this," she cried.

"Shhhh, be easy Amanda and try to stop crying. Can you do that for me please? Just try to stop crying for a second because I'm going to tell you something. Your father's upset with two people right now and he's letting his anger overflow onto you. His problem is with me and your mother. No one else and especially not you, sweetheart, so pay him no mind whatsoever, do you hear me? Do you want me to come and get you? You just say the word and I'm out the door and on my way Amanda," Silk offered.

"Yes! Please come and get me from this miserable house! I don't wanna be here anymore!" She continued crying.

"Shhhh, it's gonna be alright baby girl. I'm on my way," Silk said, hanging up and grabbing the keys to his black on black Escalade EXT pick-up truck.

"Thank you so much, Silk, for coming to get me," Amanda said smiling as she hoisted herself up into the truck, and leaned over and kissed his cheek.

"Not a problem at all, lil momma. Where's your dad at now?" he asked watching the house.

"Who fucking cares. He's probably at the bar down the street getting drunk like he does every night. He's a miserable old bastard that wants to make everybody else miserable." Amanda replied, turning her face up.

"Hey now, don't go getting yourself all upset again. I like to see your pretty face smiling, baby girl," he said touching her chin. She blushed at his compliment and touch.

Silk was a slender man who stood six-foot four-inches tall, smooth mocha complexion, with light grey eyes that all the women fell for. He usually wore his long, curly hair in French braids that rested in the middle of his back, and his dress code was fresh to death in high-end fashion by expensive designers. It had been rumored that Silk was an undercover pimp, but he always denied any allegations of it. Amanda's mother had left her father once she'd met Silk nine months ago, and had never returned home again.

"Do you want me to take you out to dinner, baby girl? he said. I know a place you like. "

"Oh my God, I'm starving now that you mention it! I'll eat anything you put in my mouth!" she giggled.

"EWW you nasty little girl, I'm going to tell your momma," he teased her.

"Who you calling a little girl? This happens to be my last year in high school, thank you very much. Hell, you're not that much older than me yourself. What are you, thirty?" she laughed.

"You hit it right on the money sweetheart, but you're still too young for me," Silk replied.

"How's that song go, age ain't nothing but a number," she sang and laughed.

"And what does your young ass know about that song?" he asked.

"Oh trust me, Silk, you'd be surprised at what all I know, and you shouldn't judge a book by its cover. You of all people should know that," she said blushing.

"Whatever you say baby girl," he replied, smiling and turning up Trey Songz on the truck's system.

☆

"After you, lil lady," Silk said, letting Amanda slide on the inside of the booth at *Houston's* on Kansas City's Plaza. "How about some filet mignon, you up for that?" he asked, giving her a quick glance.

"Are you kidding me!? That's my favorite! Hell yea, I want some, Silk!" she replied excitedly, squeezing his arm. Silk's phone rang and it was Amy.

"Hey baby, I got her with me. No baby, she's fine. Here, talk to her," he said into the phone, handing it over to Amanda.

"Hi, Mom! We're about to eat filet mignon at *Houston's*, on the plaza!" she said happily.

"Really, well aren't you special, lil miss thang. Silk left me a message saying that your dad was tripping again. You ok now?" she asked.

"Oh yea mom, I'm chillaxin big time, right now," Amanda laughed.

"Well enjoy yourself sweetheart. I've got to run errands for Silk, so I may not make it home tonight, but you're more than welcome to stay at my place. Silk will take care of you and I'll be back for sure in the morning," Amy said.

"Ok mom, well then, I'll see you when you get there. Bye, mom," Amanda said, handing Silk the phone. As Silk listened, a huge smile spread across his face.

"You got how much for me?! Oh baby, that's excellent! I'll be waiting on you when you get home. Make that money, baby," Silk said, smiling and hanging up. Silk leaned in close to Amanda's ear and whispered, "I'm ordering drinks. Do you want one?" He smiled deviously.

The ride from the restaurant was a change of pace. It was now getting dark and the night air was cool, so Silk had cracked the tinted windows and opened the moon roof. He'd switched from Trey Songz to R. Kelly as they rode, and he'd reclined his captain chair so he could relax.

"I love this truck. It's so roomy and spacious and cozy. Plus you have a banging ass system in here. The food and liquor is making me feel real chill and relaxed. Can I put my head on your lap, Silk?" Amanda asked, batting her long eye lashes.

"Go ahead, baby girl, and do your thing. I'm about to bend a few corners before we head home, so go ahead and relax." he replied, scrolling through his phone while driving.

Amanda placed her head on his thigh, resting it there snuggly. His cologne enhanced her senses now that she was so close to him, and before she'd realized what she was doing, she'd turned her nose into his crotch area and was met by his throbbing and swollen manhood bulging through his denim. She grabbed him with one hand, rubbing up and down the length of him. Oh my fucking God, she thought to herself.

"Whatcha doing in my lap, baby girl?" Silk asked, not seeming the least bit bothered.

"Nothing yet, I'm just checking you out," she replied, now squeezing his pole tightly in her hand.

"You sure that's not the liquor talking?" he continued.

"No, I'm actually not sure. But I am sure that I want to give you some head right now," she replied, now looking up at him with lusty eyes. He returned her intense stare before smiling and granting her request.

"Take him out and let me see what you can do, baby girl," he said, as he leaned back even further in his seat.

She rose up just enough to unzip his zipper and reach in for his monster member. Once she had it out she was astonished at how beautiful his manhood was. It even smelled like the cologne he wore. She held the base of his shaft and greedily sucked the tip of his dick, wanting to taste him.

"Umm" she moaned with delight, as she took him into her mouth. Her saliva was so warm and tantalizing that Silk moaned a less than manly sound as she worked up and down his shaft with her tongue, deep throating every inch of his length.

"Oh my fucking God, Amanda! Your mouth feels so good, baby girl!" Silk exclaimed while barely able to drive straight and focus on the road, now that she was going to work on him.

"Pull the truck over so I can lick your balls, too. I wanna give you the complete package so that you can experience just how good I really am," she said, as she massaged his manhood and held it close to her face.

"You just keep sucking it, while I find a spot to park sweetheart," he replied, while pulling her mouth back onto his dick.

"Umm, my pleasure, big daddy," she moaned and went back to work relentlessly. Silk pulled into a convenience store's car wash, and paid for the deluxe wash, so he could have a longer time inside the tunnel. Once inside, he dropped his jeans to the truck's floor mat and let Amanda go at his family jewels.

"Wow! Your balls even taste good and are really smooth!" she mumbled with a mouthful.

"They don't call me Silk for nothing, baby girl. You're doing an excellent job, Amanda," he replied huskily, on the brink of cumming down her throat.

She felt his balls swell and was intent on swallowing every drop of his man juice. She went back up to the tip of him and deep throated him hard and fast, now working her tongue in overdrive.

"Oh my fucking God, Amanda! Where did u learn how to suck dick like that?! This is the best blowjob I've had in years! And I got plenty bitches!" Silk exclaimed.

She giggled to herself at his compliment but never came up for air. He started to grind upward in her mouth, making her saliva roll down onto his balls. Amanda moaned while sucking him in and out of her wet mouth, intensifying his climax.

"Is your pussy wet, baby girl?" Silk asked, as he reached across the seat and slid his hand into her jeans and beyond her thong.. He found that she was soaking wet, and he fingered her tight pussy as it gripped his fingers for more.

"Oh Oh Oh. AHHH. Silk, I'm going to cum!" she moaned, grinding on his fingers until his knuckles were soaked with her cum.

Silk removed his fingers from inside her so he could taste her sweetness. Sweet candy, he said to himself. He looked down at her once more, admiring her cute and innocent face with his manhood lodged deeply in the back of her throat.

"Are you ready for me to cum now?" he asked, now grinding faster in her mouth.

"Umhm. Let me have it, daddy," she moaned looking him directly in his eyes.

"Be sure to swallow it all, baby girl. Here it comes!" he said, as his semen began to fill her mouth rapidly. He held her head in place, as he continued to erupt in her mouth.

She backed up to nurse the tip of his explosion, making sure to swallow every drop of his juice. She gave his manhood one last firm squeeze and sucked hard at his tip before raising herself up out of his lap just as the car wash's exit door opened.

"Oh my fucking God, Amanda!" Silk yelled, as she giggled and they exited the car wash.

ONE NIGHT OUT

Nicole couldn't believe what her husband Chris had just said! They had talked about doing more fun and exciting things to spice up their marriage of 15 years, and he had just come up with the ultimate ingredient, while he sat at the kitchen table and she prepared dinner.

"What would you say to us going on separate dates with complete strangers for an evening? I'd bet that would be interesting for us, honey" Chris said, while looking at his laptop.

Earlier in the day, he had probed different adult sites looking at all sorts of ads. The pictures that were attached were vivid and explicit, and it was a petite, pretty, young Asian woman that had caught Chris' eye. He'd reviewed her provocative and sexual pictures several times and decided quickly that he could spare the two hundred and fifty dollar donation she was seeking to help with her college tuition. After all, he'd been a student once and understood how tight a college kid's budget could be.

"Hmm, I agree, and I think it does sound interesting, honey, but I haven't the slightest clue who would want to go on a date with an old married woman," Nicole responded, sounding uninterested, but deep inside thrilled at the idea.

She could call her younger sister Krista and get all the assistance she'd need for such a night out. Krista had exclusively partnered with black men for as long as Nicole could remember, and had told Nicole the candid details about the different brothers that she rotated in and out of her bedroom shamelessly.

"Well babe we're not in any rush. Here sweetheart, come and take a look at some of these ads posted online. You may find someone here that sparks your interest," Chris offered, turning the screen towards Nicole.

After dinner Chris headed for the shower with a full stomach.

"Dinner was excellent darling! You're an amazing cook! Are you sure you don't want my help with the dishes, honey?" he asked before heading upstairs.

"No, babe, go and get showered and ready for bed. I'll be up shortly" she smiled. Once she heard the shower water running she grabbed the cordless phone and dialed her baby sister Krista.

"Oh my God! You're really serious, aren't you?!" Krista yelled into the receiver, completely shocked at Nicole's request for an introduction to an *available brother*.

"Oh, I'm definitely serious. It was Chris' idea for us to venture out for one night, so I'm basically just fulfilling my wifely duties and following his instructions," Nicole giggled mischievously, her face flush at the mere thought of the experience she was in for.

"Well big sister, say no more. I've got the perfect mandingo for you. Now let me tell you this, he's good at what he does. He's hung like a fucking horse and eats pussy like a hungry lesbian fresh outta jail! He'll be just perfect for your one night out! I'll call him and set it up for you asap!" Krista yelled excitedly.

"Wait! Not so fast Krista! Hold on a sec, will ya?! I at least need to know more about the guy than that! Like how about what's his first name, and how do you know him, and what does he do for a living?" Nicole exclaimed, nervously biting her fingernails.

"Oh, for Christ Sake, sis, come on! You've gotta have some faith in me here because I know what I'm doing! He's gorgeous, he's tall, he's slim, and he's exactly what you need! Who cares about all the other minor details!" Krista chuckled.

"Well, he better not be some thug, Krista! I'm serious! He's gotta be a respectable person, for God's sake!" Nicole continued.

"Oh he's respectable alright, right down to the monster of a cock he's got dangling between his legs." She replied, laughing loudly into the receiver.

"Dear Lord what am I getting myself into?! Oh, who am I kidding, I can't wait to meet him!" Nicole said, as the two sisters erupted with laughter.

A week later, Chris and Nicole's night out had arrived.

Chris had spoken to his Asian beauty several times since establishing a date, and he was feeling confident, having taken an entire Cialis tablet to ensure his night's performance.

Nicole had gone out and purchased an extremely sexy and provocative red lace bra and panties for the occasion.

At her sister's suggestion she'd held off on any prior introduction to her mystery date, as Krista said it should be spontaneous and exciting.

The brother she'd paired her with for the special occasion would meet her in the lobby of a hotel downtown, take her upstairs to a room, and ravish her until she'd had her fill.

Nicole and Chris stood face to face, in their living room before leaving for the evening.

"You look absolutely stunning babe! I oughta take you right here and now!" he said, as he hugged her and kissed her neck passionately. She wrapped herself around him, hugging him warmly.

"Thanks, handsome. You look great, too. Honey, tell me one more time that we'll be fine afterward," she said, looking deep into his eyes.

"Of course, we'll be fine. Absolutely. Are you nervous sweetheart?" he asked holding her close.

"Oh God, yes! Extremely!" she laughed, embarrassed.

"Well you shouldn't be because you're going to enjoy yourself tonight, and it'll be fun for us, I promise," he said convincingly, kissing her hard on the lips.

"Ok, I 'm ready! I can do this! Let's do this!" she screamed, amping herself up for the big event. They held hands as they headed to their garage, jumped behind the wheels of their SUV's and headed off in separate directions.

Big Marcus had gotten the call from Krista, requesting his service and expertise and had happily obliged, seeing that she was providing an expensive hotel suite and throwing in a cash incentive for him. He'd had his share of white women and knew how they craved black dick, and the extremes they'd go to get it once they were hooked.

It was ten o'clock on the nose when he'd entered the lobby of the hotel, looking for the description Krista had given him of her sister. He spotted a woman waiting patiently alone in the lounge chairs with bleached blonde hair and a dark tan. As he approached her with an extended hand, he noticed her beautiful and anxious smile.

"I'm Marcus and I'm definitely hoping you're Nicole," he said, smiling as she took his hand.

"Yes, I certainly am. It's great to finally meet you. I've heard so much about you already," Nicole replied, looking him up and down. Marcus was six four and the color of sweet toffee. His deep dimples added to his boyish appeal, and Nicole felt instant chemistry between the two of them. Not to mention the flame that had been ignited between her thighs upon contact with this beautiful man.

"Suite 220 awaits us. Shall we?" he said, as he prompted her in the direction of the elevator.

"Oh, we certainly shall," Nicole replied, wrapping her arm around his waist as they made their way to their hotel suite.

When they got to the door marked 220, Nicole went in her purse and pulled the key card out. Before she could slide it down the slider to unlock the door, Marcus grabbed her wrist. "Hold up. I forgot something," he said.

Nicole had a second of anxiety. He's changed his mind and decided he doesn't want to waste his time with an old, married woman, she thought. She started to say that it was alright, that she understood, but before she could get the words out, Marcus, who was still holding her wrist, turned her towards him, and backed her up against the door to their room.

He took her other wrist, raising them both above her head and then kissed her, hard and deep. He let her wrists go and moved his lips to her neck. She wrapped her arms around him, biting her bottom lip.

The way he was sucking and kissing on her neck had her pussy dripping wet in an instant. He slid his hand down her side, then underneath her dress, up the inside of her leg to her red, lace-covered panties.

"Fuck, yes!" she panted, breathing hard already. Nipples were *already* hard. Kitty cat was wet *already*. Yes, Marcus is exactly what the Doctor ordered, she thought, and then silently thanked her husband and sister.

Marcus slid his hand into Nicole's panties and then slid two fingers over her clit. Damn! She ain't got a man in a boat. She got a man in a fucking yacht! He pressed down on it and she purred into his ear. When he slid two fingers inside her slit she grabbed his face in her hands and kissed him, moaning into his mouth. Marcus pressed on the roof of her pussy and shook his hand in little jerks.

"Aww!" Nicole moaned loudly, not giving a damn that she was in the hallway of a hotel pressed up against a hotel suite door, with a man who wasn't her husband. A complete stranger, and a black man at that.

"You like that, baby, huh? Tell, Marcus if that feels good to you, mama," Marcus said, sucking on her neck again.

Nicole didn't think she could continue standing let alone speak a coherent sentence. Though she hadn't been the sexually aggressive type throughout the course of marriage, Marcus had changed all that up in just a few minutes time.

"Oh, yes. Oh, yes, Marcus, " she almost flat out screamed.

"What, baby? You want me to stop? Tell me," Marcus said, feeling her pussy muscles starting to squeeze on his fingers.

"No, no! Don't st-stop! I'm, I'm.. Oh, God! I 'm cumming!" And this time, Nicole did scream. As she squirted on Marcus' hand, her panties, and all down her leg and on the hallway carpet of the hotel. Once she seemed to be done convulsing, Marcus pulled his hand out of Nicole's panties, and looking at his dripping fingers glistening in the hotel light with her pussy juice, he put his fingers to Nicoles mouth.

"Taste yourself," he said. And for the first time in her existence, Nicole tasted her own sweetness, sucking on his fingers like she wanted to suck his dick.

They both turned at the sound of the light applause and whistling coming from behind them. Nicole blushed at the sight of five people who had obviously been an audience to her orgasm.

She smiled nervously, and hurriedly turned to unlock the door of the Hotel room, only then realizing that she had dropped the key card.

She bent to pick it up and Marcus slapped her on the ass earning another round of applause from the crowd as they started to disperse.

As soon as they were in their suite and the door closed behind them, Nicole pulled her dress off and pushed Marcus on the bed. It was his turn to be shocked.

"I have to taste your cock .I've never seen a black cock in real life " she said, reaching behind her back to undo the clasp of her bra.

She started to take off her panties until Marcus interrupted her, "Naw, ma', leave the panties and the heels on. And if you want this meat you got to come and get it. Show me you want this black dick."

He pulled his shirt off, and then kicked off his shoes, scooting back on the bed until his back was against the headboard.

Nicole looked at Marcus, my black Adonis for this one night out, she thought and smiled. She cupped both her titties while pinching her nipples, giving him her sexiest walk as she moved toward the bed. She undid his belt, then unbuttoned and unzipped his pants, as he raised his hips and she pulled his pants down.

His dick jumped up, still in his boxer briefs and almost hit her in the face. She looked at Marcus, who was smiling and watching her reaction. Then she looked down at his tool again and slowly reached for the waistband of his briefs.

Nicole licked her lips, then pulled his underwear down and out popped the absolutely biggest, thickest, cock she'd ever been this close to.

"I-I...I don't know if I can handle all that. Shit! I mean, I...," Nicole stammered, as she wrapped her hands around his throbbing manhood. It felt as hard as a lead pipe to her. She saw a drop of pre-cum glistening on the tip of his black cock, and found that she couldn't resist the urge another second.

She started to bring his dick to her mouth, but Marcus stopped her by pulling his meat away from her.

"Ungh-ungh. You didn't ask me," Marcus told her, smiling.

"What?!" Nicole said, her eyes still fixed on his protruding member.

"I want you to tell me what you want. If you don't, then I guess you don't really want it," Marcus said, stroking his dick in her face.

Nicole stared at the object of her hunger standing tall, just inches from her watering mouth, making her lick her lips again.

"Marcus, can I...I suck your cock?" Nicole asked, feeling hornier than she'd ever felt in her life. She never would have thought that she could ever want a man more than she wanted her husband. But she did.

"You didn't say please, and you didn't tell me what kind of cock it is that you want to suck," Marcus said, putting his dick towards her mouth and watching her instinctively open her mouth. He pulled his dick away from her again.

"Marcus, baby, please put that big, black cock in my hot mouth and let me suck it," Nicole begged, sliding a hand into her panties.

Marcus smiled and rewarded her with her prize. He let his dick go and she immediately grabbed it and brought it to her mouth.

She then went on a licking spree. She licked the underside of his dick, the left and the right. She licked his balls, and she did something that she hadn't ever done before and Marcus had never had done before. Using the underside of her tongue she licked the top of his dick, using a lot of spit.

"Yesss! That's it, baby. Get that dick nice and wet before you put it in your mouth," Marcus said, reflexively grinding his hips upward. He moved her hair from her face, bunching it in his fist at the back of her head.

"Mmmm. You like that, baby?" Nicole asked, pulling her hand from her panties and rubbing the juice from her honey pot onto his dick head.

"Yeah baby, I like that shit, now suck this dick for me," Marcus told her.

Nicole looked him in the eyes and then dove on his dick, like they had just gotten married and were on their honeymoon. She tried to deep throat him, but couldn't and gagged, which turned Marcus on even more.

When she went down on his dick the second time, he held her head in place and thrust up slightly, making her gag until her eyes started watering, then let her go. Nicole took a deep breath and wiped the tears from her eyes. Though it felt like she had damn near choked to death, it had turned her on.

Really turned her on.

"Marcus, I want you to fuck my mouth with that big, black, horse cock!" Nicole said, flipping her hair to one side.

"Ohhh! So you want to be treated like a nasty lil white ho'," Marcus said, taking her face in both his hands and fucking her mouth just like she had asked. He plunged his dick to the back of her throat like he was trying to come out the other side of her neck. His dick was dripping with spit and he was ready to beat some pussy up now.

"Come here, bitch, I want some of that white pussy. Let me see if you can fuck as good as you suck dick," Marcus said, getting up and standing at the edge of the bed with his dick in his hand.

Nicole didn't hesitate to comply. She wanted to feel her first black cock inside her more than she wanted to breathe at that moment. She lay on her back in front of Marcus, legs spread eagle.

"Pull them fucking panties to the side, bitch. Yeah, just like that. Now spread them lips open," Marcus said, kneeling down a little so he would have the perfect angle. He slapped her clit with his dick a few times, then slid it up and down her wet, pink slit. Nicole pressed her hips up, trying to get his dick inside of her.

"Marcus, please fuck me. Gimme that big, nigger dick!" Nicole said, not realizing the word she had accidently let slip.

Marcus, on the other hand, had heard exactly what she'd said and it had almost spoiled the whole night for him, but instead of slapping her all around the suite, he decided to use her slip-up in his favor.

"What, bitch!? What'd you just call me?" he said, and before she could answer he drove his dick into her tight little box. It was so tight, so wet, and so hot that he had to concentrate not to bust right off the bat.

"Ohhh, fuck!" Nicole screamed, as though Marcus had touched her cervix with his pole.

She tried to scoot back a little from the invasion of what felt like an Anaconda climbing into her pussy, but Marcus put his arms under her legs, then behind her back and lifted her up off the bed.

"It's too big! It's too big! Oh-oh-oh!" Nicole was damn near crying.

Marcus stood there banging into her with long deep strokes, thinking how her pussy was even better than her sister's. When he felt like he was getting close to busting, he pulled out and threw her on the bed.

"You nasty white bitch, you can't even take this dick. Imma make sure that pussy ain't no good to your husband when you take it back to him. Yeah, you'll be dreaming of this dick. Now turn your ass around!" Marcus commanded, slapping her little white as cheeks once she had them in the air.

He got down and ate her pussy from the back for a few minutes, and then he stood back up.

"I-I...I don't think I can take anymore, baby," Nicole said, after she had finished cumming from him eating her pussy.

"But you will," Marcus said. Then added, "I'll be easy with you this time."

Marcus spit on her asshole and watched as it slid down the crack of her ass to her pussy hole, which was already dripping wet. He placed his dick at the entrance of her backdoor and she reflexively jumped, but then settled back into position, reaching to spread her ass cheeks wide.

Marcus watched as her asshole winked at him, then he pushed his dick halfway in her ass. Nicole tried to run at first but then her sphincter relaxed and it started to feel good.

"Yes, baby, fuck this white ass!" Nicole said as Marcus pounded her. He reached around and started massaging her clit, then he drove his whole stick in her ass.

"Awwww!Fucking-fuck!" Nicole screamed.

"Whose ass is this, huh?! Whose is it?" Marcus roared, fighting not to bust his nut yet.

"It...it-it's yours, baby! This fucking white, slutty ass is yours!" Nicole yelled, as her pussy started squirting.

"And whose pussy is this, bitch? Is it your husband's? Whose white ho are you, hugh, bitch?" Marcus growled, banging her asshole for all he was worth. His balls were tightening up and he was ready to shoot.

"This is yours! Your-your pussy! I'm your ho, ohhhhh!" Nicole cried, as Marcus finally came inside her ass.

After they were done and Marcus was in the shower, Nicole thought to herself this was definitely not going to be her ONE NIGHT OUT.

CHERRY POPPER

"I'm your best friend, Sarah, for God's sake! You can trust me, now give me every detail and you better not leave anything out!!" Darcy pleaded with her roommate.

Sarah was a twenty-three year old virgin from St. Paul, Minnesota. She'd had a few close calls since her freshmen year of college at the U of M, but she'd managed to walk away keeping her sacred virginity. However, last night was different from all the other occasions, and she'd finally given in to her desires.

"Well for starters, I didn't stay over Brian's place last night, if that's what you're thinking" Sarah said, smiling, still teasing Darcy by withholding the details.

Brian was Sarah's ex-boyfriend, who had continued to linger around after they'd broken up.

"WHAT! OH MY GOD, SARAH! Well, then, who were you with?!" Darcy asked, dying from suspense.

"Ok, here's what happened last night, but you have to first pinky swear not to breathe a word of this to anyone, especially Brian because he'd be crushed. Agree?" Sarah said, holding out her pinky finger. Darcy quickly locked fingers with her.

"Agree! Agree! Now get on with the story, dammit," she replied excitedly.

"So ok, you know the black guy that's always coming into our accounting class late? The one who goes by Ace?" Sarah asked, knowing that Darcy probably didn't have a clue.

"Black guy? Ace? Sorry, sweetheart, that doesn't ring any bells for me. Describe him to me." she replied anxiously.

"He's really tall and super dark. I mean he literally almost looks blue he's so black, and he's got diamonds on his teeth and has really long dreadlocks. Oh yeah, and he plays football. Does that ring any bells?" Sarah asked, before continuing.

"Wait a minute! Hell, fucking yea! I know exactly who you're talking about now! Ugh, hello, he's fine as hell! He's always having parties at his condo downtown! His real name is Quentin and he's the star quarterback here! Duh!" Darcy exclaimed, now completely excited.

"That would be him. So anyway, last week I ran into him after class in the cafeteria, and he asked me if he could borrow my notes from study hour, and of course I said, yes." Sarah said, blushing.

"Oh, for Pete's Sake, Sarah, come on with the Juicy stuff!! To hell with the notes from study hour!! I wanna know how you ended up spending the entire night out with him, giving up your kitty cat!!!" Darcy screamed. They both laughed and rolled on the bed.

"Ok, ok, ok, so anyway, after he borrowed my notes and politely returned them, he asked me for my number, which I gave him and we started talking and texting back and forth from there.

"So anyway, the last time we were in class together he's setting directly behind me and he texts me, asking me what my favorite color is. I text him back saying that my favorite color is pink, and he texts me back asking am I sure it's not purple. I text him back saying, uh yea I'm sure, when all of a sudden I realize that I'm wearing a purple thong! And my jeans are riding so low that my thong is showing!

"My entire ass crack is out on display for him to see and I'm so embarrassed now. I turn to look back at him and he's smiling like the cat that ate the canary! So then his next text asks me if I will meet him in the stairwell in 30 seconds, and just as I'm about to text him back I hear him getting up and leaving the classroom.

"So I figured, what the hell and followed him to see exactly what he wanted me for," Sarah said, as her mind continued to recall the episode.

The stairwell door was propped open when Sarah arrived. It was so quiet in the stairwell that you could've heard a pin drop.

"Sarah, right here, behind the door," Ace called out to her, in a hushed tone.

"What are you doing back there?" she asked, confused.

Ace reached out and took her by the hand and gently pulled her into him holding her close. They now stood face to face and studied each other closely. Ace leaned in and softly kissed her lips, holding her lips with his own. Sarah's body responded as she wrapped her arms around his neck and returned his kiss.

Ace slipped his tongue into her mouth and she responded by doing the same. Ace's hands searched her body tenderly, caressing her hips and backside firmly.

Sarah held his face in her tiny palms, now kissing him passionately, her body lit on fire! His manhood grew solid, now pushing through his jeans and piercing her in her stomach.

Sarah's pussy began to moisten and contract from their making out, and she let out a moan as she felt her nipples began to harden.

Ace nibbled from her earlobe to her neck, adding to the sensations that were traveling through her body at a fast pace.

RING RING RING! The short bells sounded signaling that the class period had ended. The two froze for a moment with their lips and tongues intertwined.

"We'd better go and get our stuff before another class period starts," Sarah suggested, taking his hand and leading him from the stairwell.

Sarah and Ace walked side by side to the front of the building, neither of the two wanting to leave the other's company.

"How about we go to my place and study," Ace suggested, while pulling her into him and stealing a kiss.

"Study, huh? Is that what you really wanna do?" she asked, while wrapping her arms around his waist and returning his kiss. Ace's manhood grew firm again from her closeness and she felt him jabbing her in her stomach again.

"Yeah, that's what I'd like to do with you. You ain't scared, are you?" he asked teasingly.

"Come on Ace, what's there to be afraid of? I'm figuring that I'm in good hands with you right?" she replied, squeezing him tighter and pressing into his growing erection.

"You most certainly are, so with that established, lets ride," he said, taking her by the hand and leading her to the parking lot where his Tahoe was parked.

As they pulled into the parking garage of his downtown, Minneapolis condo, Sarah was anxious to see the inside of his place. She'd heard he was a playboy on campus, but his gentlemen-like demeanor made her feel safe and secure around him.

He grabbed her back pack, and held her hand as they walked to the elevator that led inside his condo.

Ace's twelve hundred foot condo was immaculate. Everything was neat and orderly, and his living room and bedroom furniture was decorated in a cold bone white. Even the flat screen televisions mounted on the walls in the living room and his bedroom were trimmed in white. The oil burners on the kitchen counter tops left a fresh scent of rosemary lingering in the air..

"I like your setup, and I see you're tidy too. I kinda expected to see football gear thrown about everywhere," Sarah teased.

"Thanks, I'm glad you like it, but I can't take all the credit for the cleaning. My mom slides through here at least twice a week to hook a brother up with room service," he replied slyly.

"Make yourself at home and get comfortable. The balcony's over there, the fridge is that way, and the remote to the T V is on the kitchen counter. I'm going to hop in the shower and rinse off real quick. Relax beautiful," he said, stealing a kiss from her lips and hurrying off to the shower in his bedroom.

Sarah took her time touring his place while he was gone. As she looked over the many pictures that were on display of his family, she noticed how much he resembled his mother. She stepped out on the balcony and took in the view of downtown Minneapolis, its scene of busy commuters moving at hurried pace like ants.

She caught a chill and decided to step back inside. She headed for the kitchen and grabbed a bottle of water from the fridge and returned to the sectional to plop down and stretch out across its length. A few seconds after, she heard the shower water cut off, and her name being called in the direction of the bedroom.

Ace stood in the middle of his bedroom wearing absolutely nothing, while holding a small tub of Shea butter lotion.

"Will you come here and rub some of this on my back, please?" he requested.

Sarah found it hard to breathe, after examining his entire chiseled body and the protruding member dangling between his legs. His broad shoulders, beefy biceps, veiny forearms, and washboard abs lit a flame between her thighs and instantly made her become moist.

"Sure I can do that for you," she replied nervously, barely able to audibly respond while stepping forward and taking the lotion from his hand. As she dipped her fingers into the lotion to apply some to his shoulders he spun around and pulled her into his naked body playfully.

"Can I have a kiss first?" he asked, as if not knowing the answer to his question.

"Of course you can," she responded quickly and wrapped her arms around his waist and tilted her head to the side. Ace's body was still wet and moist from the shower and the smell of him intoxicated her as she dropped the lotion when their lips locked and tongues danced in each other's mouths.

Her hands began to glide along his muscular frame, and she froze still when she held his erection in her hand.

"He could use a little lotion, too, I suppose," he said devilishly, as he prompted her hand.
Sarah bit her bottom lip as she massaged his rock hard manhood and his smooth ball sack.

Ace began to tongue her mouth passionately, walking her backward until she bumped the king size bed frame in the room. He reached down and palmed her ass, picking her up off her feet, her legs now around his waist, and climbed onto the bed with her. With him positioned now between her thighs, his raging hard on was pressing firmly against her slit, sending electric waves over her clit. She moaned aloud as he felt up her shirt, squeezing her hardening nipples while tonguing her neck.

"Take this off," he said, pulling her shirt over her head in one swift motion.

Sarah panted heavily, and her skin was on fire from his every touch. He lowered his head into her breasts, kissing them softly, while holding them gently.

"Wait, wait, wait. Here, let me help you," she said, rising up once more to unfasten her bra strap, letting her beautiful twins free. Her nipples were fully erect and exposed to Ace's warm tongue and kisses, and she nearly had an orgasm from the sensations she was receiving. Ace began grinding up and down between her thighs, making her snatch completely soaked. Sarah reached down and unbuttoned her own jeans.

"I'm ready for these to come off now," she breathed heavily underneath him, wiggling to get the jeans around her wide hips.

Ace snatched the denim off and threw them to the side of the bed in one motion and resumed his position between her warm thighs. His hard rock dick was now piercing through the crotch of her wet thong as he continued grinding into her. With her arms around his neck, she returned his thrust, grinding back up at him while looking directly in his eyes. With her legs spread wide, he reached down and pulled her soaked thong to the side and stroked her wet and swollen love button with his fingers.

"Ohh, ahh, umm, " she whimpered, writhing her hips as he inserted his fingers into her hot and wet slit.

"Damn, baby, your coochie's really tight, and I like that a lot," he said as he pushed her thighs open wider and slid down the bed until his lips were resting on her love mound. He then parted her rose petals and took her clit hostage in his mouth, tugging and rolling his tongue over her sensitivity in slow and deliberate circles.

"Ohh, umm! I'm going to cum, Ace. Unhh! I'm cumming! Please don't stop!" she squealed, and bucked her hips, keeping her thighs wide as he pushed his mouth into her sopping wet slit while she orgasmed. Her legs shuddered as she felt her cum rushing out uncontrollably.

He continued to lick at her clit, flicking his tongue and lapping up her sweet juices.

"Turn over and get on your knees for me," he commanded.

"I may need your help because my legs are still shaky right now," Sarah replied in the aftershock of the climax that had just ripped through her body.

Ace leaned in and kissed her passionately, and for the first time she tasted her own sweetness.

"I got you, baby, you're in good hands," he whispered in her ear, before flipping her over onto her stomach and pulling her waist up until she was on her knees. He then pushed the small of her back down until she was fully exposed to him.

He massaged her healthy backside before parting her slit and plunging his tongue inside of the wetness as far as it would go.

Sarah felt faint from the overwhelming sensations he was causing her entire body to experience. With Ace's hands firmly holding her in place, and his tongue working in overdrive in and out of her pussy, Sarah collapsed on the bed and attempted to squirm away.

"Oh, oh, oh, Ace, please, I'm tingling everywhere!" she moaned, her juices leaving a trail across the bed as she tried to slide away from his relentless tongue.

Ace politely ignored her pleas and wasn't letting her slip away. He got ahold of her again, and this time parted her from behind and drove his tongue directly into her ass.

"Ahh! I like that!" she moaned excitedly. She reached back and held her ass apart for him and climbed back onto her knees, giving him all the access he needed to tongue fuck her asshole.

He worked his tongue in deeper and deeper, now striking her hole with precision.

She bucked her hips backwards and began meeting his tongue eagerly with her own thrust. She buried her face into the blankets and yelled at the top of her lungs as she climaxed again and collapsed once more onto her stomach.

"Holly shit, Ace! What are you doing to me!? I can't quit shaking all over!" she exclaimed out of breath and face flushed.

"Trust me, baby you'll be fine. I got you," he replied smoothly, and rolled her onto her back.

As Ace went to part her shaking legs, Sarah's quivering asshole broke wind, and was heard by both of them. Ace immediately started laughing and fell back away from her, fanning the smell of the fart away from him.

"It's not funny, Ace! And you'd better stop laughing! It's your fault!" Sarah replied, embarrassed, but also laughing." Oh no, mister, get your ass back over here! You're going to finish what you started," she continued, chasing him across the bed and climbing on top of him.

Now in this position, she stared him directly in his dark brown eyes and melted.

"Ace, I've been saving myself for the right guy, and well anyway, at this very moment I believe without a shadow of doubt that it's you, Ace. So please be gentle with me, ok?" she said, never breaking eye contact.

Ace didn't respond with words, but instead started kissing her passionately and placed her on her back. Now between her legs again and continuing to tongue her wildly, he drove his nine inches of manhood straight up into her, until he could go no further and his balls rested on her still warm asshole.

Sarah's legs wrapped around his waist tightly and she completely froze. Pain and pleasure displayed on her flushed face. Ace had felt her cherry pop, and he kept his dick lodged deeply inside of her as her walls contracted around him.

"Open your eyes, baby. Look at me, Sarah," he softly coached her. Sarah's eyelids opened slowly as she stared up at him innocently.

"Now I want you to breathe easy for me," he continued, kissing her lips gently, and now beginning to move his swollen pole inside of her." You're doing just fine for me baby. Are you ok?" he whispered.

"Uh huh, " she replied, as a single tear fell from her eye.

"I want you to keep relaxing and get comfortable with me being inside of you," he said, taking both her hands and joining them with his, holding them above her head. Ace kissed her neck and earlobes softly and pressed into her gently.

She finally allowed her body to fully relax, getting comfortable with him being inside of her. She responded by kissing him back passionately and sucking his bottom lip into her mouth. She reached behind him and smacked him hard on his backside, the sound echoing off the bedroom walls.

"I think I'm ready now," she growled sexily.

"Are you sure, sweetheart? I mean I don't want to hurt you," he replied.

She slapped his backside again, giving him the green light to proceed.

As Ace pulled a portion of his length out, he looked down and noticed traces of her blood at the base of his dick, before he took a deep breath and commenced to stroking her tight virgin pussy like a madman.

He leaned in and roughly sucked her lips while pinning her legs against her shoulders and banging her pussy hard and fast and deep.

"AUHH. Ummm!" Sarah yelped, eyes shut tightly, as he drove himself into her relentlessly, pounding her snatch.

"Whose pussy is this?! Huh? Tell me, Sarah," he asked sternly while stopping and stirring his dick inside of her from side to side.

"AUHH! It's yours, Ace!" she cried out in pain.

"Louder, Sarah. I want you to say it louder!" he commanded.

"IT'S YOURS, ACE! THIS IS YOUR PUSSY!" she screamed, now completely relaxed and getting in to it and slowly bucking her hips up at him. Ace rolled her over, never removing himself from her tight box.

"I want you to ride my dick hard and fast. Just how I like it. Can you do that for me, baby?" he asked, reaching up and taking her breast into his mouth. She leaned forward and fed him her nipples, becoming more and more relaxed with him being inside her.

She rose up and down slowly, getting used to the length of him before getting jiggy with it. Ace reached around her and palmed her ass cheeks firmly and drove himself deeper into her.

"Here baby, let me help you ride this dick. Are you ready?" he asked taking ahold of her ass and not waiting for an answer from her before continuing. He thrust upward into her warm split while pulling her down onto his rock solid manhood.

"Does this hurt, or feel good to you, baby?" he whispered in her ear, almost bringing himself to an explosion inside of her warmness.

"UMM. AHHH. Both! It hurts but it feels really good, too!" she replied as her climax mounted.

"I'm ready to cum, but are you ready for me to?" he asked, his balls filled and ready to blast.

"Oh, yes, yes. I'm ready to feel you cum inside of me!" she moaned and came down harder onto him meeting his now desperate thrust.

"That's my baby girl! Here it comes! AUHH!" he grunted, pulling her hips down onto him and holding her in place, lodging himself inside of her warm tunnel as his semen gushed and filled her contracting walls.

"Oh Sarah, that was the best I've ever had, baby!" he continued as he finally relaxed and she dismounted him. Sarah lay beside him breathing heavily now, flushed and spent.

"Baby, go and grab a towel from the bathroom to clean me up with" Ace ordered, now folding his arms behind his head and stretching his long frame across the bed.

Sarah glanced down at his still semi-erection as it laid on its side, covered in both their juices and traces of her blood.

The sight of this aroused her immensely and savagely, and she became instantly wet, and before she knew it, she'd dove in between his legs and tongued the tip of his dick.

"Ace baby, you don't need a rag. That's what my mouth is made for," she replied as she stuffed her throat with his meat, hungrily sucking and licking him off. She looked up at him while she went to work, seeing if he was enjoying the job she was doing.

Ace grabbed the back of her head and began to drive himself deeper into her throat while she continued to slurp and suck him off as fast as she could.

"Good job, baby. Keep sucking my dick just like that and I'm going to cum in your mouth. I want you to swallow all of it for me, baby," Ace said huskily.

"Umm, fuck my mouth, Ace," she moaned. Sarah looked him in his eyes wanting to witness the pleasure she was bringing to him. Soon she began to taste his sweet and salty cream spilling into her mouth as she worked her tongue like a tornado up and down his shaft.

"Swallow all of it, baby," he said and grabbed her head as he exploded into her mouth.

Sarah swallowed as much of his juice as she could before backing up for air.

"Holy shit, Ace! That's certainly a tummy full!" she exclaimed, while holding his manhood next to her face. Ace laughed as he let off the remaining shots from his load.

"Yea baby girl, the second one's always bigger than the first, making it the best one. Remember that," he replied as he slid out of her grasp and relaxed back on the bed.

"Will you hand the remote over on your side of the bed, please? I wanna catch the highlights before we go another round." he said with a smile of satisfaction.

SHOW BOAT

~~~~~~

"Honey, I'll be down in just a second," Amy called out, as she took one last look in the vanity mirror in their bedroom. She blew her reflection a kiss, primped her hair and then headed down stairs.

"Carl, honey, how do I look?" Amy asked, posing at the bottom of the stairs for her husband.

It was Carl's fifty-fourth birthday and Amy was hoping that it would end in some steamy sex, though she had her doubts, since Carl couldn't seem to keep any kind of an erection for any longer than ten minutes at the most. Carl, on the other hand, knew that the years were finally catching up to him and not being able to fully please his wife sometimes put him in a bad mood.

Not today. It's my gawdamn birthday, for Christ sakes and I mean to enjoy it. I've been waiting for this for a few years now, and by God, I mean to enjoy it, Carl thought as he looked at his beautiful wife, posing for him and smiled.

"You look beautiful, Amy. Hell, you look twenty years younger than me, that's for gawdamn sure," Carl said, clipping his cell phone to his belt, then turning to get the keys off the end table by their couch.

"You are so full of it, Carl. I am three years younger than you are and I'm sure I don't look too much younger than that, but thank you anyway, you handsome man, you. Oh, and Carl, dear," Amy said, as she stepped out onto the porch, "I'm not wearing any panties. Just a garter."

Carl almost dropped his car keys at that little piece of information. He regained his composure and stepped out of the house, locking the door behind him.

"Amy, do you know how long I've been waiting for this," Carl asked, as he climbed into their Ford 250.

"I know, Carl. You've been talking about this same boat for at least two years now. I honestly began to think that "boat" may have just been the code name for some younger woman you might've been having an affair with," Amy said, smiling. "At last, you're finally going to get it and I am finally going to see it. Happy Birthday, honey!"

"Thank you, hon, but let's not forget that even though it's my birthday, this gift is for the both of us. You're going to love it, just you wait and see," Carl said, turning up the volume of the country music coming from the radio.

"I'm sure I will, Carl," Amy said, placing her hand on his thigh and giving it a squeeze. Amy turned to look out the window and enjoyed the view. What I'd love is to get my boat rocked or however the young people say it these days, she thought and smiled.

Carl parked His Truck in Front of the BOATS-R-US store. Before getting out he looked over at his wife, "Amy, just remember that this is just as much for your pleasure as it is for mine, honey. Yours even more so, though," he said, kissing her lightly.

"Awww, thank you, dear. That's sweet, but it's your birthday and I'm happy as long as you enjoy it," Amy said, taking his face in her hands and planting a kiss on his lips with a smacking sound.

"Oh, I'm definitely going to enjoy this, don't you worry about that," Carl told her, then gave her a devilish wink as he got out and waited as she did the same.

They entered BOATS-R-US hand-in-hand, both smiling.

Amy, who had never before been in the store, was surprised at how big it was. It was the size of an airplane-hanger and it also had a second floor.

The first floor was filled with medium-sized boats of all types. Gleaming, polished wood and shining stainless steel was everywhere. The boats and the way the showroom lights reflected off of their different surfaces took her breath away and made her feel ten years younger.

Amy was so captivated that she didn't realize that Carl had stopped at the front desk and spoke to someone.

"Come on, honey, the one we're looking for is up-stairs. We'll take the elevator," Carl said, placing his hand in the middle of her back as they left the desk.

Amy was surprised to feel her husband's hand slip down lower, until he was just about palming her backside. She glanced at her husband and he just smiled and winked at her again. If this is what these boats do to him then maybe I will like the boat, she thought, adding a little more swing in her hips. As they reached the elevators, one of them dinged and the doors opened.

"Hey, Carl, my man! I was wondering if you were serious. I was just getting ready to clock out for the day, but Vincent, at the front desk buzzed me and told me you were here, so I thought I'd come down to meet you. And this must be the extremely lovely wife. Hellooo, Mrs. Sanderson. My name is Andre," Andre said, taking her hand in his, but instead of shaking it, he brought it to his lips and kissed the back of it. "And it is a pleasure to make your acquaintance."

Amy was at a loss for words. I've never seen a man as handsome as this in my life, she thought, as she tried to calm the electric tingle that Andes's kiss had sent through her body. Andre's mocha skin, baritone voice, thick lips, corn row braids, and sculpted physique, clearly visible through the white button-up shirt he was wearing, was enough to make Amy's knees weak, face red and nipples hard.

"I...excuse me. Um, it's nice to meet you Andre. And, uh, you can just call me Amy," Amy said, thinking she needed to get control of herself.

This young man can't be any older than thirty-five at the most; he's young enough to be my son, if, of course, I was a black woman, she said to herself. Amy looked over at Carl who was standing there smiling.

"I hope you enjoy seeing your soon to be new boat. I also hope it pleases you especially, Amy, because it would make my day to be able to give pleasure to a woman as beautiful as yourself," Andre said, as he put his hand in the middle of her back, where Carl's had been only moments ago.

"I'm going to tell you Dre, buddy, my Amy definitely deserves to be pleased. Lord knows I haven't been up to the task for a couple of years now," Carl told Andre, clapping him on the back as they all stepped into the elevator.

"Carl!" was all Amy could say. She was so surprised and embarrassed, that she didn't think she could get any more red. It felt to her as if she were blushing all the way down to her toes.

"I'm telling you now, Carl, if I was in your shoes, I'd be at home right now, with a face full of my wife's pus-, uh, excuse me, Amy," Andre said, giving her an embarrassed smile. Amy felt his hand slide down a little more, until it was resting on the base of her spine.

"Hey Dre, you know it's my birthday. Hell, tempt me not, buddy, 'cause I might just give you my shoes for the day. I'm sure Amy could use it," Carl said, laughing.

Amy had had enough. If Carl wants to keep embarrassing me, then two can play this game, she told herself.

"Yeah, Carl's right. I definitely could use that and a whole lot more! I'm serious, you guys, the more you talk about it, the more I'm thinking of sneaking off into one of these boats and pleasuring myself! Unless, of course, a certain husband was willing to let a certain handsome young man assist me," Amy said, laughing, putting her hand on Andre's shoulder.

Before any of them could say another word the elevator dinged and the doors slid open. The trio stepped out and headed through the store to and area labeled: **SHOW BOATS**.

They walked past different boats of various sizes and shapes until they were standing in front of a sleek, high-glossed black boat, with the name painted on the side: **BIG AND BLACK**.

"Oh my! It's beautiful," Amy said, unconsciously wrapping her arm around Andre's waist.

Carl was smiling. Amy realized that Andre was running his hand up and down her back. The fact that Carl didn't say anything about Amy being touched so intimately by another man, and a black man at that made her feel a little more bold and daring.

"That is exactly what I'd like to experience, something big and black," Amy said, stepping up to the boat with an extra switch in her hips again.

"Well, now that you say it, that would be a better birthday present than me getting ten boats! What do you say, Dre, my boy? Would you mind helping your old pal and letting my wife see what it's like to have something big and black? I'd owe you one, buddy," Carl said to Andre, with a conspiratorial wink.

"Carl, my man, I'd be more than happy to. Though, it would be up to your wife," Andre said, walking up behind Amy and pressing his body against hers. He put his hands on her hips.

Amy was so shocked that she didn't know if she accurately understood what was being said. She felt something hard poking her in her tail bone. That can't possibly be this young man's cock, Amy was telling herself, until her thought was interrupted by her husband's voice.

"I'm just gonna go on back down and finalize the transaction on my boat, honey. Why don't you stay up here with Andre and, um, enjoy yourself," Carl said, and with one last wink for Andre and a kiss for Amy, he turned and headed back towards the elevators.

Andre didn't waste any time. He reached one hand into the front of Amy's dress and inside her bra, and with the other hand he moved her hair from her neck and placed a kiss on her shoulder.

Amy felt like she was in a sex movie.

She was so excited and turned on that she thought her nipple might poke right through Andre's hand. She wanted to turn and find her husband. Tell Andre she didn't think she should or could do this, but the truth was she'd needed a good lay for two years now and she was already melting in this young man's hands. Not to mention she had never had sex with a black man except in one of the wildest dreams of her young life.

Carl gave me his blessing he wanted this for me, probably had even planned it. I'll be damned if I don't be a good wife and enjoy it like he said, Amy thought, reaching her hand behind her to feel that bulge that was poking her and getting bigger.

"Yeah, that's right...let me know you want it...," Andre said, kissing and sucking on her neck.

"Oooh! Yes, I want it! I need it!" Amy said, taking his hand and bringing it to her mouth. She sucked on his first finger, then added the second finger. Amy gobbled Andre's fingers like a dick and he wanted to watch her work his pole like that, so he pulled his fingers out of her mouth and stepped back, slapping her ass as he did so.

"Let's go on in the boat and finish this," Andre said, unbuttoning his shirt.

"God! I thought you would never ask. I want to see it and then I want to taste it, and then I want to feel it in me...deep!" Amy said, pulling down the top of her dress to free her breasts as she followed Andre up onto the boat.

They stepped into a small room, fully equipped with a bed and dresser. Andre was out of his pants in a blink and sitting on the edge of the bed, stroking his thick, ten-inch pleasure pole.

"Yessss! That is some cock you got, Andre," Amy said, pinching her nipples as she started to get down in front of him.

"No, Amy. Get up here on the bed with me, cause I wanna eat some of that pretty, white pussy, while you suck this dick," Andre said, laying back on the bed with his dick sticking straight up, like a space ship ready for take-off.

"I haven't had my kitty licked in I don't know how long, since Carl doesn't really do it unless he's drunk and then he doesn't really drink either!" Amy said, getting on the bed and turning around.

She straddled Andre's face then bent and grabbed his dick. She couldn't wrap her hand around it, so she used both of them to stroke his hard dick. Andre waited until he felt Amy's tongue take its first swipe of his dick head, then he spread her pussy lips, and stuck his tongue as deep in her tight hole as he could.

"Oh, my lord! Ahhh!" Amy cried, then tried to stuff her mouth with his big, black fuck stick.

Andre sucked on her dripping, tight hole, then her pussy lips, and finally her clit, sticking a finger deep inside her gripping womb. He finger fucked her and sucked her clit until she started to shake.

"Holy fuck! Yes! Yes! Don't stop! Ah-ah! Ahhh!" Amy screamed, as she came.

"Yeah, that's it, cum on my tongue, baby! Mmmm-hmmm," Andre told her.

After Amy had stopped convulsing, Andre slapped her ass cheeks, leaving red hand prints and causing her to flinch and moan.

"Now, turn that ass around. I want you to sit on this dick. Take your dress off first," Andre said, as he reached over the edge of the bed and pulled his wallet from the back pocket of his pants. He opened the wallet and took out a condom, then put the wallet back in his pocket.

"Ungh-uh. I want to ride this horse bare back. I'm gonna enjoy every second of this, young man," Amy said, taking the condom out of his hand and tossing it on the floor.

Andre just smiled. I'm going to fuck the shit out of this old vixen he told himself. "I like that. Now get your ass over here and take a ride on Big and Black," Andre said, smiling and stroking his throbbing member.

Amy stood up on the bed, then lowered herself sexily over Andre's dick. When the bulging head of his pulsating pipe parted the lips of her hungry snatch, he thrust up hard and fast.

"Unghhhhahwww!" Amy screamed, feeling like she was being split in two, which was the best feeling she'd felt in years.

Andre wrapped her up in his strong arms, laid back on the bed and banged into her warm, tight twat with a vengeance. His balls slapped up against her ass in a loud rapid sequence.

"Mmmm-hmmm! This what you been needing, ain't it!" Andre said, pumping in and out of Amy's pussy like a hydraulic drill. "Is it? Huh? Talk to me."

"I-oh-ahhhh-y-yes! Yes, I need it!" Amy said, barely able to speak. She hadn't been fucked like this in her entire life.

Andre continued to pump in and out of her creaming cunt, then slapped her ass again and let his dick slip sloppily out of Amy's creamy pussy. "Gimme some of that pussy from the back," he said, wiping sweat from his forehead with the back of his hand.

"No, I want you to fuck me up my ass. Please put that big, black dick in my tight ass!" Amy said, surprising Andre. She looked back at him as she rubbed her pussy, getting her finger wet with her juices and then pushing that finger in her asshole.

Andre couldn't believe his luck, but he wasn't going to stand there and waist time not believing it, when he had some tight white ass to fuck. He spread her ass cheeks wide and spit, dead center, on the winking, brown eye of her asshole.

"You ready for this, Amy? Imma give you exactly what you been missing. Yeah, you're gonna love this black dick," Andre told her, as he placed the head of his cock at the entrance of her waiting back door.

He grabbed a handful of her hair and wrapped it in his fist, pulled her hair, causing her to look towards the ceiling, and pushed into her sucking sphincter.

"Ahhhhh! Ahhhh-oh-gawd!" Amy screamed at the top of her lungs.

"Oh my fuckin shit! This ass is good, Amy!" Andre roared, slapping her ass with his free hand.

Andre pounded Amy's tight asshole until he felt his balls start to draw up and tighten. He squeezed his eyes shut and tried to think of anything but the fact that he was at work, fucking the wife of one of his customers in her ass.

"I'm going...ahwww!"Amy cried, sticking two fingers inside her dripping pussy, "I'm cumming! Oh, yesss! I'm cumming!" Just then, Amy did something she had never done in her life, only heard of. She quirted. A stream of hot liquid shot out of her pussy, soaking her hand, the bed, splashing Andre's balls and dripping from them onto his legs. This sent him over the edge.

"Ahwwww!Fuuuuuuck! Turn around. I want to cum on those titties!" Andre growled, voice tight from the strain of trying to hold his nut long enough for Amy to slide off his throbbing, dripping cock.

Amy spun around as fast as she could with weak legs and a burning ass, "I wanna taste your cum! Cum in my mouth! Come on give it to me!" Amy said, kneeling in front of him, aiming his rigid, slick rod at her open mouth and pumping it furiously with her hand.

"Here it comes here it-awww-ohshiiit!" Andre screamed, as his dick started spurting stream after stream of his hot cum into Amy's waiting mouth.

Amy let Andre shoot four blasts of his cum, the first going along the side of her nose and onto her check, the next three going straight to the back of her throat, before wrapping her lips around his dick head and flicking her tongue over the tip of it, urging every last drop of cum out of him. When it seemed he was finally done she let his still semi-erect tool slip from her lips.

"Oh shit! That was good!" Andre said, falling onto the bed.

Amy lay down next to him to catch her breath, then she remembered her husband whom she had completely forgotten about. Hell, she had forgotten she was even married. Amy sat up to gather her clothes together and saw Carl standing there in the doorway, smiling.

She started to say that she was sorry, and didn't how it all happened and a list of other things, but before she could get a word out Carl spoke.

"Soooo, do you like it, hon?" Carl asked, without really having to, because he could clearly see the satisfaction written on Amy's face under the shock of thinking she'd done something wrong.

"I...I-I...well, yes. I did. A lot!" Amy said, embracing the situation.

"That's good, because it wouldn't be much of a show boat if you didn't. Isn't that right, Dre," Carl said, smiling at her and giving Andre a wink.

NO STRINGS ATTACHED

"Fuck you, Brad! I'd rather walk home than ride with your pathetic ass! I can't believe you're that much of a fucking pig to do something like! You've ruined my entire night, asshole!" Heather screamed at her boyfriend as they stood out front of the sports bar they'd come to for the evening to watch the Floyd 'Money' Mayweather fight.

Heather had excused herself to go to the ladies room, only to return and catch Brad adding their waitress' phone number to his cell phone.

"I'm sorry, sweetheart! I don't know what I was thinking! You know how I get when I drink! Please, Heather, don't be mad at me, I'm sorry, for Pete's sake!" Brad pleaded with her.

"I'm not getting in your car. You can forget that! I'll find my own ride, Brad. I sooo hate you right now for doing that to me!" she continued, and started walking away from him.

"Heather, wait dammit!" he said, going after her. As he reached for her arm, Heather skipped away, and with anger fueling her reflexes, she spun around sharply and slapped him hard across the face, breaking one of her French tips.

"Fuck, Heather! What's wrong with you?! Why you gotta be such a fucking cunt? I said I was fucking sorry and you still wanna make it into a big deal! Well fine, walk your fucking ass home because obviously you need some time to cool off anyway! You fucking cunt!" he shouted and stormed off leaving her standing in her tracks.

"Fuck you too, Brad! You'll regret this night long before I will, asshole!" she yelled at the back of his head.

A few moments later, Heather saw his Mustang turning out of the parking garage of the Legends Mall, his tires burning rubber, leaving her behind.

A devilish grin spread across her face.

"Yes! It worked!" she yelled to herself. It had all been a setup and Brad had taken the bait.

When Heather went to the ladies room, she'd found their waitress for the evening and gave her a twenty dollar tip to go and flirt with her boyfriend Brad. Heather would then *conveniently* stumble across the two of them flirting, which would then create an enormous fight and scene, leaving Brad to go home without her.

Heather intended on staying behind to get to know the twin brothers who were setting at the bar that had caught her eye. From the very moment she'd entered the establishment she'd been drawn to the very attractive pair, and had been making very sexually suggestive eye contact with the two throughout the evening, when Brad was watching the fights. At one point during the evening, when Brad had been so preoccupied with cheering and watching the fights, Heather had wandered near the bar.

When Andre saw this he quickly moved within earshot of her. "I'm not one for games, snow bunny, so I'm going to cut to the chase. I definitely like what I see, and me and my twin bro wanna get to know you. So what's up, you gonna shake your date and come get on one with me and bro?" Andre asked casually, coolly sipping his drink and smiling at her.

"I'll see what I can come up with, handsome," she smiled mischievously, backing into him teasingly, before she headed back to her table.

Andre and Andrew were known on K.U.'s campus as the "Splash Brothers." They were twenty-two year old twin brothers that were party animals and attended the college on full basketball scholarships. They were tall, with light complexions, and fresh-faced with mesmerizing light hazel colored eyes that made all the girls melt. The two prided themselves on how many girls they could bang in three way scenarios, and tonight would provide them with yet another locker room story.

Game on!

The sports bar was packed to capacity, leaving only standing room available near the bar area.

"Oh shit, bro! Don't look just right now. That thick ass white girl from earlier is headed this way," Andre said to Andrew. Andre was the more outspoken and aggressive of the two. Andrew turned slowly just in time to catch the view of Heather as she boldly sashayed through the crowd, making her way over to the two. Heather's walk exuded a sexy confidence saying that she was totally in control.

"Well, hello, you two very handsome men! It's so good to officially meet y'all! Do you mind if I squeeze in here?" she said, while budging between the two men seductively.

"Not at all, go right ahead, sexy. In fact, now the party can begin. We've been waiting for you. I'm Dre and this is my bro, Drew. And your name is?" he said with his hand extended to her.

"My name is whatever it needs to be for the night, sweetheart. I'm more than sure the two of you handsome and very attractive men are wonderful guys and all, so please don't be offended, but tonight is strictly no strings attached." she replied and moved her hand across his broad shoulders.

"No strings attached, huh. I like that a lot. So does that mean that anything goes?" Drew interjected slyly moving in closer to her until she was sandwiched between the two.

"Exactly, lover boy. No limitations. Everything and I do mean *everything's* fair game tonight fellas," she replied sexily as she ran her palm up Drew's pant leg. Dre knocked back his sixth shot glass of Ciroc and leaned into her face until they were nose to nose.

"So I hear what you're saying, and it all definitely sounds like music to my ears, but I want you to understand that when we leave here, it aint gonna be no fronting or faking, you understand that? So this is your chance to back out right now before my dick gets any harder than it already is," Dre whispered while taking her hand and guiding it to his bulging erection stuffed away in his jeans.

As she discreetly rubbed and massaged him through his jeans, her nipples stiffened at the thought of him inside of her.

"Oh my, this is very nice. I can't wait to feel every inch of it. And I'm assuming the two of you are identical, too," she emphasized and looked back at Drew. Drew flagged the bartender over.

"What'cha drinking, I'm buying" he said politely, staring into Heather's lust filled eyes.

"Honey, they don't serve what I wanna drink back there. Come on and let's get outta here shall we. I'm fucking horny!" she exclaimed excitedly, her statement taking Drew by surprise.

Heather took them both by the hands and led the way to the bar's front doors.

Once outside, the night's breeze seemed to enhance the sexual tension amongst the trio, and along their stroll to the parking garage, Dre and Drew groped Heather's voluptuous body, squeezing her plump rear end and feeling her breasts and erect nipples that were protruding through her halter top.

By the time they reached the elevator doors leading to the parking garage, Heather was tonguing Drew with her hands down the front of his jeans, while Dre was grinding on her ass from behind.

Once all three boarded the elevator and the door had shut behind them, Heather went into immediate action, dropping to her knees in front of the twin brothers.

"I want a dick in my mouth, now!" she demanded, as the elevator began to rise.

Dre was the first to get his belt unbuckled, and with lightning speed he buried eight inches of his manhood deep into her throat while gripping the back of her head.

Her mouth was warm and welcoming as she took all of him in and out of her mouth, deep throating him and resting the tip of him on her tonsils.

"I wanna see those pretty green eyes baby. Look up here," Dre said. Heather responded to his request by going all the way down on his pole and then pausing, looking up at him sexily with a devilish smile before continuing.

She then pulled back, taking his dick entirely out of her mouth to spit a large amount of saliva onto his tip before shoving him back into her throat, never breaking eye contact as instructed.

Drew's jaw dropped in astonishment, watching her in action. The elevator ride was over and it was now time to exit.

"You're next, handsome," Heather said to Drew as she stood and dusted off her knees.

"Dre, I'm getting in the back seat with Heather. After seeing all that, I don't wanna wait for my turn," Drew said to his brother as they slapped fives.

No sooner than Drew had sat in the backseat, Heather had her face buried in his lap.

"Pull your jeans all the way down so I can get those balls, too, baby boy," she said sucking him completely into her wet mouth and deep throating him.

Drew complied and gave her the access she needed to lick his balls while she went into overdrive, stuffing them into her mouth greedily.

Dre had opened the opposite car door, wanting in on the action. "Get those pants off, and get up on your knees, and poke that ass out, so I can fuck you while you suck my brother off!" Dre ordered.

Heather moved with precision, never breaking stride, with Drew lodged deeply in her throat, pulling her pants down to her ankles and getting to her knees in the back seat so that Dre could take her from behind.

Heather's wet slit glistened in the parking garage's lighting as Dre prepared to enter her doggy style. He dipped his ring and middle fingers into her fuck hole first, and she responded, backing all the way down to his knuckles as he fingered her.

"Whatever you're doing back there to her, bro, keep doing it, because she's sucking the hell outta my dick over here!" Drew shouted.

"Roger that! I'm getting ready for take-off!" Dre replied, pulling his fingers from her box and replacing them with nine inches of man meat. Dre held her waist as he entered her from behind, sinking slowly into her wetness, stroking her long and deep.

"OOUUHH! YEAA! UMMM!" she moaned as he bottomed out inside of her.

"Do you like that? I'll bet you do. Throw it back harder if you like it, baby," Dre said huskily as he sped his stroke, and slapped her pale ass cheeks.

Heather began to buck wildly, her walls getting wetter and contracting around Dre's pole. Dre responded by pounding her deeper and harder, and sinking his thumb into her tight asshole, bringing her climax to a head quickly.

"AUUHHHH! I'M CUMMING! AUHHH!" she screamed in passion.

Drew's balls erupted into Heather's mouth as he grabbed her head and shoved his dick into her throat. "You worked for it and here it cums! AUHH!" he exclaimed, releasing a flood of hot cream into her mouth. Dre continued to pump her from behind and finger her asshole until he could stand no more and had to explode, pulling out of her hurriedly and blasting her backside with his load, bringing the trio's no string's attached evening together to an end.

JESSICA TO THE RESCUE

"DAMN YOU MATT! YOU ALWAYS FUCKING MAKE ME DO SHIT THAT I REALLY DON'T WANNA DO! ALL BECAUSE YOU OWE SOME DAMN DOPE DEALER MONEY!" WHEN ARE YOU GONNA GET YOUR SHIT TOGETHER?" Jessica screamed at Matt, knowing where the conversation was leading,

Her boyfriend Matt had a serious problem with drugs, and whenever he was deep in debt and feared for his safety, he'd ask his steady girlfriend Jessica to *smooth* things over with who he owed the money to.

"Jessica! My back's against the fucking wall here! I mean come on, for Christ's sake, you know I wouldn't ask you if I really didn't need your help with this, honey!" Matt exclaimed, nervously looking out of their bedroom window.

Matt's nerves were on edge, as he'd been up for the past three days snorting coke and downing vodka. He owed money to one of the most brutal and notorious drug dealers in L.A. and had to make a payment soon, or suffer the consequences.

"How much is it this time, huh? One thousand, two thousand?" Jessica went on.

"I'm in deep this time, baby. Almost four grand," Matt replied, never making eye contact with her because he was still hawking the cars that rode up and down the street.

"WHAT IN THE FUCK WERE YOU THINKING? YOU FUCKING IDIOT! HOLY SHIT, MATT! WHERE ARE YOU GONNA COME UP WITH THAT MUCH MONEY? I CAN'T FUCKING BELIEVE THIS!" she screamed and covered her face, mind racing about the situation he'd just pulled her into.

"Look, here's what I need you to do: first, I need you to go get as much money as you possibly can from your bank. Then, I'm going to give you his address, and you go by there and drop off the money, and tell him that I'm outta town but you're making a payment for me, at my *instruction*, and that I'll take care of him as soon as I get back in town. That'll buy me a little time to figure out what I'm gonna do to come up with the rest of it. You got me on this Jessica? Because, honey, if there was ever a time that I needed you, it would certainly be right now," Matt said, now looking her seriously in the eyes.

"Matt! I only have maybe a thousand dollars in my checking account until I get paid again next week!" she screamed, as she burst into deep sobs.

"Honey, just give it to him for me, will ya? It's saving my life here, because if I don't come up with something fast, there's gonna be a bunch of black guys surrounding the house demanding their fucking money," Matt said, coming to her and taking her into his arms.

"Ok, ok. I'll do it! But I swear to God, Matt, if you do this shit again, I'm leaving your ass! You got that?" she said through her weeps and sobs.

"Honey I won't ever do this shit again! I swear on a stack of bibles, I won't honey!" he said through clenched teeth.

"Where do I have to take the money to? I'd better get going before it's too late. I gotta be at work early again tomorrow," she said.

"I have the address written down where I go to meet him. I'll go grab it for you. He goes by C-Night, and don't forget to tell him that I'll be by there as soon as I get back in town. Tell him I had a family emergency or something like that, ya know? Make it sound real for me, baby," Matt said as he went to grab the trap house address for Jessica.

C-Night had just sent his two lil homies home, after they'd been posted in the trap with him for several hours, helping him with the flow of traffic that the pure cocaine he sold brought in.
Business was excellent for him at his new location, with the exception of one of his newly hired workers named Matt, who seemed to have disappeared suddenly.

C-Night had no worries though, because he was deeply connected in the streets, and those who worked for him certainly understood his status as an O.G. Crip in L.A.

After the house was cleaned up, and all the contraband was concealed, C-Night turned off the porch light, signaling to any potential customers that business was done for the day. Now alone, he relaxed, kicking off his shoes and stretching out across the leather sofa in the living room.

Just as he began to nod off into a dream, he heard footsteps and then a knock at the front door. C-Night immediately reached for the 40 cal. he kept in case he encountered any suckas, and headed for the front door.

"If the light's off on the front porch, then that means don 't knock on this fucking door!" he boomed, clutching the heavy weapon tightly, peeking through the peephole.

"Hi. Uh, sorry. My name's Jessica and I'm supposed to find a guy named C-Night at this address. I need to talk to him about my boyfriend Matt," she said nervously, holding up the piece of paper with C-Night's name and address scribbled on it.

C-Night snatched the door open and was momentarily taken back by her beauty. Jessica had shoulder length brown hair, and strikingly blue eyes. The thin blouse she wore revealed that she was braless, and the night's air had firmed her nipples to a point. The blue jeans she wore were snug, creating a slight camel toe that suggested that she wasn't wearing under clothes at all.

He stood in silence, sizing her up before he spoke.

"So Matt sent you here, huh. Well, where is he at? And why did he send you instead of coming himself?" C-Night asked sternly.

"Are you C-Night?" she asked, still very nervous.

"Yea that's me," he replied sharply.

"Well see, Matt went outta town because he had a family emergency, and he asked me to drop off some money he owes you, and to tell you that he'll be back in town in the next few days to take care of the rest of his debt," she answered, finally making eye contact with him and returning his stare.

C-Night's bronze skin tone, light brown eyes, and perfectly white teeth made him easy for her to stare at.

C-Night finally relaxed and stepped aside, giving her the green light to step inside of the trap.

Jessica stepped into the house and immediately smelled the aroma of marijuana. She saw the gun in C-Night's hand and her heart jumped into her throat. The speeding up of her heart rate caused her nipples to get even harder.

He noticed her reaction to seeing the weapon, noticing how her nipples were protruding a little more. He went back to the couch and sat back down, purposefully not offering Jessica a seat yet. He had seen a lot of shit and been in a lot of situations in his life, so the thought that she could possibly be the police or be wearing a wire popped into his head. Though he doubted it, he'd rather be safe than sorry. He sat the gun on the coffee table in front of the couch.

"Are you the fucking police? Or the Feds? You wearing a wire, huh?" he asked her sternly.

"N-no! I'm not stupid. Listen, I just want to give you this money and leave. I don't want any problems," Jessica said, voice shaking.

"Yeah. If that's all you want, then strip," C-Night said, leaning back on the couch and lighting a cigarette.

"What? I - I," Jessica started saying, but found that she couldn't think of anything that she could say that would convince this man.

"You're what? Wearing a wire? Is that what you're doing? You and Matt, trying to jam a brotha up?" C-Night said, sitting up on the couch.

"Hell, no! I wouldn't do anything like that. Listen, if I take my clothes off, you're not going to rape me or hurt me or anything are you? You'll let me pay you and leave?" Jessica asked, thinking how crazy she was for letting herself be put in this situation and how much more crazy she must be to be getting turned on by the whole idea of getting naked in front of this man, who was obviously some sort of big time drug dealer. A gangster, even. I 'm insane she thought.

"Rape you? Ha! You gotta be high and outta your mind. C-Night aint gotta take no pussy," he said, and had to laugh a little at that.

"Okay, Okay, I'll do it," Jessica said, and pulled her shirt over her head releasing her nice and perky, C-cup breasts. Then she unbuttoned and unzipped her jeans, kicked off her shoes and took off her pants.

C-Night had to admit to himself she had a nice body. He could feel his dick start to harden and noticed that Jessica looked down at his lap before looking up at him again. He leaned back on the couch.

"So, whatcha got for me?" he asked her, taking a puff from his cigarette.

"I got, well, I got a thousand dollars, but like I said, he's," Jessica exclaimed, until C-Night interrupted her.

"He gave you one funky ass thousand to give me when he owe me four racks!" he said, angrily. "Imma kill em, disrespecting me like that!"

"Jessica sat down on the love seat, still naked. She didn't know what to do. She hated Matt for putting himself let alone her in these situations time and time again. But she didn't want him to be killed.

"Please don't! I'll - he'll figure something out. I'll help him out with whatever I can. Please, I'll do anything," Jessica said, feeling desperate.

C-Night looked at the cute white girl sitting bootyhole naked and unconsciously grabbed his dick.

Jessica saw the movement, noticing the outline of what looked like a monster of a cock, and felt her pussy tingle. She had an idea.

"Is there anything I can give you or do?" she asked, still nervous. She opened her legs.

"Huh. Well, that all depends on what you got to give and how good it is," he said, thinking if she was serious, he would blow her shit out. He sat there and watched as Jessica thought it over for a second and then got up, moved the coffee table, and knelt down in between his legs.

She kept her eyes glued on his crotch as she reached up and massaged his hardness through his jeans, then undid his pants, pulled them down a little, and then pulled his dick out.

"Oh my fucking gawd!" she said, holding his dick in a hand that barely wrapped around it.

"What's up baby? That aint what you used to, huh?" C-Night said, smiling at her reaction to the sight of his manhood.

"Don't worry though cause you gone get acquainted with it tonight. Go ahead, baby, do ya thang."

And she did.

Jessica sucked first on the head of his dick, swirling her tongue around it while it was in her mouth, then going down as far as she could.

"Damn, girl! Shit!" C-Night said, surprised.

"Mmmm, hmmm," Jessica mumbled, keeping his dick in her mouth, while she looked up at him. She stuck her tongue out as far as it would go, his dick still in her mouth, moving it side to side along the bottom of his shaft as she sucked him at the same time.

"Ohhhh! Shit, yea! That's some boss head for a boss brotha, right there," he said, toes curling in his socks. He put his hands in her hair, held her head in place and grinded slowly upward into her hot mouth.

Jessica was enjoying sucking his dick now, so she relaxed her throat muscles, gripped his dick behind his balls, pushing as much of his meat down her throat as she could stand.

"Holy! Muthafucka!" C-Night said, squeezing his eyes shut. He felt he was on the verge of busting a nut, so he pulled his dick out of her mouth. Jessica took a few deep breaths, then burped as C-Night stood up and let his jeans drop to his ankles. He sat back down, kicking his pants off as he did.

Jessica stood up, squeezing one of her titties and rubbing her clit. She had only intended to suck his dick, but now she told herself that she would just ride him a little bit and that would be that. She got on the couch, with her feet planted on the outside of his thighs, reached down and held his dick, then slid down on it.

"Fuucckk! Oh, oh, oh!" she screamed, wrapping her arms around his neck as she bounced up and down on only half of his dick.

Time to turn up on this bitch, C-Night told himself, as he put his arms under her thighs, then stood up, sliding all of his rigid pole inside of her in one fluid motion.

"Gaaawwddamn! Bitch, this is some good pussy!" he exclaimed.

"Oooh! Fucking mother fucker, I'm cumming!" Jessica cried, as C-Night pounded her pussy with short, quick strokes like a jack hammer.

"Yeah, bitch. Oh yeah! Uh-huh. That's what black boss dick makes you do," C-Night growled, pumping Jessica's tight pussy. He turned towards the couch and sat her down.

"Now turn around and hike that ass up," he said, grabbing his heater and moving it to the coffee table behind him.

"Okay, baby," Jessica said, getting in the doggy position. C-Night didn't waste any time pushing into Jessica's asshole.

"Oww! Wait!" she screamed in pain, trying to scoot off his dick. The way he had her positioned balled up in the corner of the couch, there was nowhere to run. She had done anal with Matt, but his dick was considerably smaller than C-Night's and she had been ready and prepared for it.

"Just relax, girl. You said you'd do anything. You wanna save Matt, right? Yeeeah, that's it! Take this dick," he said, smiling.

"Okaaaay. B-but he, he doesn't o-owe you after th-this, right?" she moaned, starting to rock back and forth on his dick slowly.

"That's right. Now throw that lil white ass back at me, baby," C-Night said, moving a little now. He started to pump harder, and reached around to play with her clit.

"Yes, baby! Oh, fuck yes!" Jessica screamed, rocking back now meeting him thrust for thrust. She heard her pussy hiccup, releasing pent up air around C-Nights cock. C-Night felt the hot air blow past his dick and that sent him over the edge.

"Okay, okay," he roared, pulling out of her ass and grabbing his dick with a master grip, "turn around bitch, now open ya mouth."

Jessica turned around and barely had time to think he's really gonna make me taste my own ass, before C-Night's dick plunged into her mouth and he was squirting his cream down her throat.

Jessica gagged a little at the taste of her butthole, but that was a small price to pay for Matt's life.

She swallowed in big gulps as C-Night continued to erupt into her mouth.

Finally, when she'd felt his explosion subside, she looked up at him.

"Did I earn Matt's safety with you?" she asked with a pleading look in her eye, still holding him in her hands.

"You most certainly did, Jessica," he said looking down at her with satisfaction.

Jessica was thrilled to hear that Matt was safe now, and to show her appreciation she took him into her mouth once again, bringing his erection back to full attention.

"Good! Now I feel like celebrating!" she mumbled in between slurps.

SCHOOL DAZE

"Mr. Parker, this is the third time this week that you've been late for my class. Now, either you must be the President's newly recognized son and so, have diplomatic immunity or you just don't like my class."

"Naw, Mr. Br-," James started to reply, but was cutoff when the teacher held up his hand, palm out as if to say stop, and started back in on him again.

"In either case, Mr. Parker your attendance, lack of effort, as well as the way that you're late arrival interrupts the rest of your classmates' lessons, is indeed unacceptable," Mr. Brown said, as James made his way to his desk, took his book bag from his shoulder, and started to sit down, smiling at a couple of his friends.

"Yes, yes, indeed. Please do have a seat Mr. Parker so we can get back to this chapter on the human anatomy. Only not at your desk. No, why don't you go have a seat in the principal's office," Mr. Brown told him, looking over the top of his thick glasses, and down his nose at James.

Some of the students whistled, a couple oohed, and someone even said damn. This was bad. James' smile melted instantly. Shit! Not the principal! He thought.

The high school had just gotten a new principal a few days earlier and James had missed her introduction to the school because he had been suspended, but it was said that she was a mean white woman from down south, who had zero tolerance for problem students. Shit!

James stepped into the principal's outer office and was in the domain of the principal's secretary. Ms. Neeman was a sexy, dark skinned woman with light brown eyes.

She was twenty-four and she and James shared a secret that they both did a good job pretending didn't exist.

The secret was that they had met on Facebook right before the school year started. James, who had been lifting weights since he was fifteen (two years and some change now) had posted some pictures of himself on Facebook lifting and flexing for the camera.

He also posted that he was twenty-five, which was a lie. Not knowing who Shelia (which was Ms. Neeman's first name) was at the time, he sent her a friend request. She had accepted it and as their Facebook conversations started to progress she had told him that she figured he was around twenty-five to twenty-seven.

This was also a lie. Long story short, they decided to meet at a motel that she had picked (purposefully choosing one on the outskirts of town so it was less likely that she would be caught going to a motel with some young boy) telling herself that it would be just a one-time thing. This too was a lie. But, their sexapade had come to a screeching halt when he had walked into her office, accompanied by his parents to be enrolled for school.

The damn boy did have some good things going for him. For one, he was fine as hell, he did have a nice chiseled body, and shit, she couldn't deny it, the boy had a big ass dick that he definitely knew how to use.

Oh, and the most important thing was he could keep a secret, she thought now as he walked up to her desk.

"Hey, Ms. Neeman."

"Good afternoon, James. Go ahead and have a seat. The principal will be with you shortly," she said. Then added as an afterthought, "She's, well, she's something else, but she's alright."

"Can you put in a good word for me or something because I ain't trying to get expelled! You and her cool, right? Come on, look out for me this one time, Ms. Neeman. Please! I mean, I'll pay you or something. Whatever you want!" James said, knowing that if he got expelled, there went graduation, and with his graduation went his car that would be following right behind it. His parents would make damn sure of that. He was definitely desperate right now.

"I don't know what I could say James. Yeah, me and Jacky, I mean Mrs. Reed, is cool, but," Ms. Neeman said, looking sad and sounding apologetic.

James was going to try and plead his case one more time, but just then the door to the principal's office opened and out walked a short white woman in a grey two piece business suit. She was pretty with red hair that was pulled back in a tight ponytail that came down to the middle of her back. She was wearing a white blouse underneath her suit top and you could tell she had very large breasts.

"You must be the sometimes present, and usually late, and very interruptive James Parker. I am your new principal, Mrs. Reed. Of course this is all news to you I'm sure, since it seems you were," she paused for a second to look at a piece of paper she had in her hand, "yes, you unfortunately were suspended at that time." She shook her head at that bit of information, then said, "In my office, James."

He walked past her and stepped into her office, glancing at his watch as he did. 2:47p.m. Hopefully she's ready to go home to her husband, if she has one, and relax, that way I might have a chance of getting off with just a warning, he thought.

Mrs. Reed was all business. She pointed at him and then at the chair in front of her desk. James dropped right in the chair without a second's hesitation.

He stole a glance around the office and saw a picture on her desk of her, a fat man, and a little girl that looked like a younger version of Mrs. Reed. So, she is married. But how the hell dude's fat ass pull her, he asked himself. James took a chance and turned in the chair to see if she was maybe standing there waiting for him to say something and saw that she was leaning on the secretary's desk, slightly bent over talking, and it sounded to him like they had just shared a laugh.

Damn! It looks like she even got a big booty on her too, he thought and had just started to admire the thickness of her thighs when she looked back and saw him looking at her ass. He turned around so fast that he damn near spun out the chair. He could've sworn he heard more laughing.

Then from right behind him in the door way Mrs. Reed said, "I might just have to try that Ms. Neeman! And that of course was a joke."

James sat in the principle's office with the door closed, looking everywhere except at Mrs. Reed.

Mrs. Reed on the other hand had spoken on the phone to Mr. Brown, called her husband and told him she would be home late due to a 'problem student.' This was the only time she had looked at him since she had come in and sat at her desk. He looked at the clock. 2:53p.m.

Just then the bell rang and the secretary's voice came over the school's intercom speakers, **"This ends today's classes for all students. After school detention for the day is canceled. Any students who were scheduled for detention today will report tomorrow morning before home room to the**

principal's office to check in at the secretary's desk. Have a nice day."

Five minutes after that message and he was still sitting there. Now ten minutes. The phone rang and Mrs. Reed answered, said a few words and then told Ms. Neeman to have a nice day and she would see her tomorrow.

She looked up finally and said, "So, James I'm sure you have a cell phone, but if not feel free to use this phone and call your parents or guardian to let them know that you will be staying late today for disciplinary reasons. If they would rather hear it from me, I would be more than happy to explain."

"I have my phone but, Mrs. Reed, please don't expel me. I -," James said, but she cut him off.

"What I decide to do or not to do will be based largely on your performance here today, James. Now make the call. "

He made the call and had to listen to his mother tell him that if he got suspended one more time he could just hand his car keys over as soon as he got his ass back home.

After she hung up and he put the phone back in the pocket of his book bag, Mrs. Reed got up and took her suit jacket off, then draped it over the back of her chair. She came around her desk and went to the door, opened it and looked out, then closed it and locked it.

What the hell? James thought.

She sat on the edge of her desk facing him, letting her heels drop off her feet, then hiked her skirt up a little and leaned forward with her hands on the table between her legs. James tried not to look, but couldn't help but glance at the amount of leg that was exposed to his view. That, plus a good helping of cleavage. Though he was nervous that didn't stop his dick from jumping in his pants.

"James, James, are you bored here or is there something else that you find more interesting," she said this and leaned back, placing her hands behind her for support, and opening her legs slightly. James couldn't respond and he also couldn't believe what he was seeing.

"I do not believe it! Are you looking up my skirt, young man?" she asked.

This got through to him, "No, I, I was," he started to stand up and retreat out of reflex, but realized too late that since he was wearing sweat pants, that was the worst move he could have made.

"I was! That's what you just said, isn't it? So, you were! And oh my, is your dick getting hard, too?" she said, sliding off the desk and moving toward the chair he was sitting in.

James instinctively tried to cover his dick, which was going flat almost as fast as it had gotten hard. He just knew that not only was he getting expelled, but he was also going to jail or maybe prison.

"Mrs. Reed, please, I'm -" he started to say, but again she cut him off.

"There's no excuse for your actions. The only way that this situation can be resolved is, well hell, you saw mine so drop them," she said, unbuttoning her blouse, which he failed to notice because of the shock of what he thought he heard her say.

"What?"

"I said drop your pants. You saw under my skirt, and now I get to see under your pants," she said, walking up to him, blouse unbuttoned and hanging open, giving him a clear view of the black lace bra she wore.

Now, it finally hit him, and James' dick had caught on. He decided he was going to enjoy this.

"But since I couldn't really see nothing, it wouldn't be fair unless you let me get a good look at what you got under your skirt and take your shirt off, too. And to keep it fair," he pulled his shirt over his head and threw it in the chair.

Mrs. Reed didn't waste any time either. She knew what she wanted, so she pulled her blouse off and reached behind her and unclasped her bra and let them both fall right where she was standing. James pushed his pants down to his ankles and his dick jumped out of the slit in the front of his boxers.

"Oh, damn!" Mrs. Reed said.

Before James could say something slick about how she still had to take her skirt off, she dropped down in front of him and started sucking his pole like he never had it sucked before. She cupped his balls in her hand and fondled them while she tried to deep throat him. She gagged, pulled his dick out of her mouth, and slapped her face with it. Then started to lick and suck his balls.

"Gawdamn! Mrs. Reed, shit!" was all he could say, as he watched her go from his balls to his dick and back. She stunned him when she spit on his dick, then started stroking it with her hand.

She looked up at him, "You have a really big cock, James. And," she sucked it into her mouth, pulled back slow and, when it came out of her mouth, it sounded like a bubble gum popping.

"You like that, James? Mmmm," she said, stroking his dick again, "It's my turn now."

She stood up and sat on top of her desk. She pulled her skirt up and started to take off her panties, but he stopped her.

"Naw, leave 'em on. I want it just like that," he said, hooking his arms under her knees and pulling her closer to the edge of the desk. "I got this."

He pulled her panties to the side, noticing that she had a nicely trimmed patch of red hair. He spread her pretty pink pussy lips open and tried one of his tricks; he spit right on her clit.

"Grrrrr! Yes, spit on this pussy" she growled, which made his dick get even harder. She reached around her own legs and held her pussy lips open for him.

"Now, eat that shit!" she commanded. And he did just that, doing everything he had done on Sheila during the summer. He even tried some of the things he saw on the porn movies he'd watched.

When it was all said and done, he had to pull her back towards him three times because she had scooted damn near off her desk.

He positioned his dick at the entrance of her pussy, pulled her titties out of her bra, then plunged in.

"Oh shit!" They both yelled at the same time. Him, because her pussy seemed so tight and hot that he had to fight not to bust a nut right then on the spot. Her, because she hadn't had anything in her that big since she had given birth to her daughter.

They fucked all around her office; on the floor, in the chair, against the wall, up against the door, and they ended up on the floor, her on her knees ass up, face down.

"Oh, shit Mrs. Reed, I'm bout to cum. I'm bout to-" he said, thrusting away. He started to pull out.

"Cum inside me, baby! Cum inside me!" Mrs. Reed screamed.

The last thing James remembered was looking at her puckered asshole. Then he exploded. When he came to...

The sun was going down. The sky was that pinkish color it gets when the evening has decided it's going to clock in for the day. He fumbled with his car keys, looking over his shoulder at the school and saw Mrs. Reed just coming out of the front doors looking like she was in the same condition as he.

She waved. He waved back. Then he got in his car and left the school in a daze.

PISS TEST

~~~~~~

Quincy pulled into his driveway, parked and got out of his car. He stretched, then went to the mailbox and peeked inside, saw nothing, then went in his house. He dropped his keys on the coffee table and then went to take a shower.

"Damn! I was supposed to go see my parole officer today," he said out loud.

He snatched up his cellphone on the way to the shower and dialed the parole office number. No answer.

Fuck! It was after five o'clock anyway so what did he expect. He left a message.

He knew Karen, who was a snobby suburban white woman, was gonna be on some bullshit. He smiled at that thought as he got in the shower.

She couldn't trip too much though because he had a job now and the only reason he'd forgot to call her was because today was his first day at the job. Hell, she's been sweating me about a job for the whole two weeks I been out of prison, so hopefully the bitch would chill her chubby ass out now that I'm working, he thought.

Quincy got out the shower and decided to celebrate his first day of working. He sat on his couch and rolled up a blunt, still in his towel and leaned back.

His cell rang and he looked at the screen, saw it was Lisa, a female he met last week and answered. They talked for a minute and she told him that she wanted to come see him. He told her to stop at Prize Package and get him something to eat on her way over, then hung up.

He put on a porno, kicked his feet up on the coffee table, and hit the weed. He was half way through the blunt when someone knocked at his door. He smiled as he got up from the couch thinking Lisa must have burnt the rubber off of her tires to get here that fast. He opened the door wearing nothing but a towel, blunt in his hand and looked into the face of Karen, his parole officer.

"Uh, let me get dressed real quick, Karen, cause I just got out of the shower. It won't take but a couple of minutes," Quincy said, hoping to at least get some time to flush the blunt that was still lit and smoking in his hand.

He went to close the door, but Karen stepped inside the house looking him up and down.

"No, that won't be necessary, Quincy. I can see that there's a lot more going on here than you just needing to get dressed. Is that marijuana that I smell? Hell, the way the smoke is pouring out I'll probably have a contact high," she continued.

Once inside the house she looked around, thinking that it was actually a nice house for a single man. Then her eyes landed on Quincy's chest, scrolled their way down to his abs, and then the towel. She looked up quickly, hoping that he hadn't noticed how her eyes had been roaming and where they had roamed to.

She closed the door behind her.

Fuck! I'm going back to prison was all Quincy could think. He went to the coffee table where the ashtray was and put the blunt out. Hell, there wasn't any sense in trying to hide it now. Then he saw the porno going full throttle on the flat screen, and lastly the sound finally registered to his ears.

He mentally shook his head. Karen must have heard it at the same time because she frowned and came around to see exactly what he was watching.

What she saw made the color rise in her cheeks and it also made her nipples get hard. Real hard. A white woman was sucking a black man off while another black man was pumping her from behind.

She cleared her throat. "Uh uh. Let me get this straight —" She tried not to look at the screen again, but couldn't help it. "You were supposed to call me today, but instead you decided to do what? Sit at home, smoking weed, watching -" she stopped mid-sentence, glanced at the screen again and realized she was breathing a little harder than normal, "watching porn, and hell, probably masturbating!"

She looked at the screen again for a little longer this time and Quincy noticed it and reflexively looked, too.

"Whoa, Karen. I wasn't jacking off for one, and for two, I didn't get a chance to call you cause today was my first day at work. When I got off and realized I was supposed to call you, I called your office and left a message," he said, noticing that she was still looking at the porno.

He saw that her nipples were hard and that she was blushing. He couldn't help but wonder if she was getting wet from watching the porno.

She was a little chubby and about twenty something years older than he was, but on the whole she was still cute. She turned to him again and noticed he was looking at her ass. She looked down at the towel again and saw a bulge there. Oh my, she thought.

"I'm gonna need a U.A. from you, right now," she said, pulling a U.A. cup out the plastic bag it was sealed in and handing it to him. "Where's your bathroom?" she asked, pulling out a form, then undoing the buttons of the jacket she was wearing.

"Umm, the bathroom's right over there, but I just used it when I got out the shower," Quincy said, stalling.

"Well, I suggest you find a way to squeeze something out because if you refuse, that's considered a positive test. In other words, a dirty. So, after you," Karen instructed him, then followed after him, stealing another glance at the porn movie still going strong.

Quincy stepped into the bathroom and turned to see where exactly Karen was standing. Right in the doorway. He thought that was odd, being that she was a *female* P.O. If she was going to piss test him, she was supposed to have a male officer with her.

Something was up with her. Whatever she had been on when she had showed up at his door, he was willing to bet that it was something entirely different now.

He took the top off the cup and then started to pull his dick out, when Karen came all the way in the little bathroom and positioned herself where she could see him. Yeah, she's on something Quincy said to himself. He reached in his towel and loosened it enough that it fell to the floor when he pulled his dick out.

"Ho-ly shit!" Karen said in a breathy tone.

"This is what you really wanted when you came over here, ain't it, Karen?" Quincy asked, taking a chance.

"Yes," Karen whispered, not taking her eyes off the prize.

"Show me what you wanna do with it then. Sit down on the toilet and put it in your mouth," Quincy told her, taking his dick in his hand and stroking it.

"Yes," Karen said, and sat down like he'd told her.

Quincy stepped in front of her and she took his dick in one of her hands and cupped his balls in the other. She stroked his joystick a few times then looked up at him. "If you tell anyone about this and it gets back to me, I'll find something to violate your ass for and I'll ask for the high number too. And I'll get it," she said, then licked the head of his dick like a lollipop.

She did that a few times and then dove on his dick with vengeance.

She even deep throated him and stuck her tongue out, and licked his balls at the same time. Before he knew it she had him backed up against the bathroom wall and was kneeling in front of him. She looked up at him, then spit in her palm, stroked his dick and sucked on the head.

He couldn't hold out any longer and told her he was about to cum, thinking she wouldn't want it on her, but Karen surprised him even more, by keeping his dick in her mouth, unbuttoning her blouse, pulling her titties out of her bra, and then holding them up for him like he was a king and she was presenting him with an offering.

His dick came out of her mouth with a loud pop!

Then she put her mouth back on it and pulled back again so that when it came out it made that same popping sound. Then Quincy *popped*, shooting cum all on her chest and titties. Before he was done cumming, Karen grabbed his dick and put it back in her mouth, swallowing the last drops.

Quincy leaned his head against the wall. That was one hell of a piss test, he thought smiling.

SLEEP DON'T CUM EASY

~~~~~~

"What's wrong, honey, are you having trouble sleeping again?" Rachel's husband Danny asked, while they lay in bed. Recently it seemed to Rachel that Danny had lost his ability to stimulate and please her sexually. Night after night she climbed into bed with her husband silently hoping that he wouldn't want to have sex with her, her frustration having grown after countless attempts of failed climax, yet having to fake an orgasm. Her pussy throbbed to the point of her nearly being in tears as she longed for pleasure. Sure, she could masturbate as plenty of unsatisfied housewives do, but even that was starting to lose its luster.

The time for some action was now!

"Hello, yes, I'm looking for a personal trainer. May I speak with someone who can help me?" Rachel asked into the phone. She'd decided to call first before heading over to the gym that night.

"Would you prefer a male or female mam?" the receptionist asked.

"Well, actually, I'd prefer a male. Thank you for asking," she replied.

"Ok then, hold for one moment and I'll get a trainer on the line for you," the receptionist said.

"This is just what I need! To get outta this damn house and get some new dick!" Rachel thought to herself.

"Hey, what's up? This is Ted. How can I help you?" A masculine voice spoke into the phone.

"Hi, my name is Rachel Molver and I'm looking to start working out with a personal trainer who can give me a workout somewhat later in the evening. You see I'm having trouble sleeping, it may be anxiety, who knows, but I figured that if I exhaust myself physically, later in the evening I might possibly sleep better. Does that make sense to you?" she asked hoping she didn't sound too silly to him.

"It makes perfect sense to me, mam. Have you been into our gym for an initial assessment before?" Ted asked.

"No I haven't as a matter of fact, but I can come in if I need to," Rachel replied quickly.

"Alright, well I'll be in the gym until around ten o'clock tonight. You can pop in whenever you'd like before then." Ted said.

"That sounds perfect to me. How does nine thirty sound?" she asked.

"Nine thirty it is, then. I'll be looking for you. Just have whoever's at the front desk page me and I'll be right with you," he replied, enjoying how easily clients fell into his lap.

"Well alright then! And by the way, I'd appreciate if you called me Rachel, please. The whole mam title makes me feel old," Rachel said with a chuckle.

"Not a problem, Rachel. I'll look forward to meeting you this evening," he said before ending the call.

Rachel's brain went into overdrive as she sat contemplating her night at the gym: Holy fuck, he's black. I've never been with a black guy before! What if he's got a huge, big black dick like the ones I've seen in the pornos? Oh, my God!"

"Well, honey, I'm certainly glad to see you exercising. I think it'll be good for you, actually," Danny said in a matter of fact tone as Rachel dressed for her appointment at the gym.

"Honey, you're the best! Thanks for supporting me with this!" Rachel said as she retrieved his credit card and put it in her purse.

"Go gett'em, tiger!" he said, smacking her on her backside as she headed out the door.

Rachel noticed that when she pulled into the gym's parking lot there were hardly any cars parked in sight, and wondered to herself where everyone was at. She parked and turned on the dome light to add another coat of MAC lip gloss to her pouty lips.

"Here goes nothing," she said. Taking a deep breath, she headed inside.

The inside of the gym was enormous. The weights and machines seemed to be scattered everywhere.

"Where are all the people?" she questioned herself, noticing that there was no one at the front desk.

"Rachel, is that you!" Ted shouted from the upper tier of the gym. Rachel's eyes quickly darted to where the voice came from, as she squinted trying to make out the image.

"Yes, it sure is! Do you want me to come up there?" she yelled back.

"Nope, just hang right there, I'm coming down!" he yelled back at her, heading her way.

They studied each other as they approached for the first time.

Rachel was immediately pleased. Ted was tall, dark, handsome and buff. Just like the black guys in the pornos.

"Hello, and nice to finally meet you. Follow me, if you will, over to my desk so I can get your measurements," Ted said leading the way.

Along the way Rachel continued to study him from head to toe. Especially his backside. She wasn't used to seeing much of that back at home. He's built like a mechanical bull, she thought to herself.

As he typed her personal information in his computer, the inevitable but necessary question came about.

"And how old are you Rachel?" Ted asked routinely and nonchalantly.

"Do I really have to answer that question?" she giggled.

"Only if you want me to train you," he replied, giving her a warm smile.

"Well, you tell me first how old you are, then," said Rachel.

"I'm twenty four, going on twenty five. Now, see how easy that was? Now it's your turn," he said, continuing to smile, revealing his perfectly straight and white teeth.

"Okay, Mister Ted, I'm forty eight, almost forty nine. There, are you satisfied?" Rachel replied, as if she was ready to get on with his so-called assessment.

"Not quite yet, but I will be when you stand up and take off your jacket for me so that I can get your measurements, please," Ted said while wheeling his chair over to her side of the desk.

She stood as he requested and the view from standing over him while he sat directly in front of her made her mind instantly create a sexy scenario with his face buried into her womanhood. Rachel was beginning to become moist and wet as her pussy was starting to contract.

"Do you want me to put the measuring tape around your thigh, or would you prefer to do it yourself? Ted asked, smiling politely at her.

"Oh please, by all means go right ahead. I'm not that shy," she replied, giggling while watching him intently.

He charted all her measurements and quickly and stood. "Now you're ready to step onto the dance floor with me," he said and took her by the hand and led her out into the gym.

Rachel lie flat on her back, while pushing the universal bench press, flexing her small C-cup breast.

"Oh my! I can really feel that! How many more should I do?" she asked.

"That's it for now. Let's move on over to the machine that helps tone your lower half," Ted, said pointing at the quad, hamstring, and hip flexor equipment.

Rachel strapped her thighs into place and pushed with her inner thighs, spreading her thighs as wide as they would stretch apart.

Ted's eyes darted between them, getting a quick glance of her camel toe print through her elastic pants.

Rachel noticed him sneaking quick peeks so she spread her thighs, holding them apart for seconds longer, poking her mound out further for him to see, and on her fifteenth rep a surprising Charlie-horse shot up her inner thigh at lightning speed, causing her to let the weights slam down as she jumped up from the machine, screaming in a panic and fell to the floor.

"Oh God, Ted, help me, please!" she screamed.

He quickly dropped to his knees and immediately took her leg into his hands and kneaded her spasming muscle while holding one leg spread apart from the other.

"Is this working? Has it stopped yet?" he asked, concerned.

A look of complete satisfaction and relief was displayed across Rachel's face.

"Yes it's working, alright, and what you're doing feels really amazing, actually. You don't suppose I could pay you to use those hands on my entire body, do you?" she asked flirtatiously.

Ted smiled at her comment, not yet understanding exactly who he was dealing with.

"We actually have someone on our staff that I hear is really good at giving massages. She has a chair in the back by the sauna, and though she's not in right now, I'd be happy to set you an appointment with her," he replied.

"No, Ted, I want your *hands* and no one else's. The way you just rubbed my thigh let me know that you should be a massage therapist, plus a trainer!" Rachel said, complimenting him.

"Well I certainly appreciate the compliment, Rachel. Here, let's get you to your feet," he replied and pulled her up.

As she stood up she could see the imprint of his penis through his sweat pants. She quickly looked around the gym making sure no one was in sight and went for it, grabbing a handful of his manhood and stroking him through his sweat pants.

"This looks amazing, by the way," she whispered as she came closer.

"Damn, lady! You're bold as hell!" Ted said in shock, as if she'd lost her damn mind grabbing his dick like that. A slight smile spread across his face as his manhood began to respond to her touch.

"Baby boy I'm horny as hell, and from the way it feels you are, too," she said as she continued to massage his erection firmly.

Ted stared at her awkwardly for a brief moment before taking her by the hand and leading her to the steam room in the rear of the gym. Once inside, he grabbed her face firmly and sternly and looked into her eyes, wanting to get an accurate read on the situation he was in.

"So what's your story, lady? Are you one of those white women who can't get enough black dick? Huh? You went black and you ain't going back?" He continued staring her down, his eyes serious and piercing into her as her mind raced.

"No, no, no! Not at all! I've never even been with a black guy before!" she pleaded, not knowing what his next move would be.

"Yeah, is that right!? Lady, I see your type all the time out here in Overland Park! You rich white bitches can't get enough black meat!" Ted screamed in her face and pushed her away.

Tears immediately fell from her eyes, now feeling embarrassed and rejected. As Rachel began to leave the steam room Ted reached out and grabbed her by the arm, pulling her into him.

"Where the fuck do you think you're going!?" Ted said in a growling tone.

"I thought you were upset and didn't want me. I was going to leave," she said through sobs.

Ted leaned in and sucked her neck roughly and ran his hands down the inside of her elastic pants, digging in between her ass cheeks. Rachel's body anxiously wrapped around his as her pussy instantly came alive. She went into overdrive returning his kisses frantically, as she moaned from the mounting pleasure she was experiencing.

He stuck his fingers into her hot and pulsating pussy roughly and her juices overflowed quickly onto his knuckles. Ted fingered her hot box faster while continuing to suck all over her neck.

"Oh, oh, oh. Fuck, Ted, this feels good," she moaned in passion.

Ted snatched his fingers from her slit and abruptly stuck them into her mouth.

"Lick my fingers clean. Yeah, just like that," he said, holding her face with one hand firmly.

As she slurped his fingers greedily, she reached for his hardness protruding from his pants.

"Will you fuck me now, please?" she begged in between slurps, staring intensely into his eyes.

"I might, but what are you going to do for me?" he asked in return.

"Whatever you want me to do, honey" she moaned with her eyes closed.

"Is that right, huh? How much money do you have for me?" he questioned.

"A lot, daddy! Can you please fuck me now?!" she begged.

"What's a lot?" He continued to torment her overheating pussy.

"I have two thousand dollars. Is that enough, daddy?" she asked.

"Hell, muthafuckin yeah! Bitch, hurry up and get them clothes off your ass!" he said as he helped her strip down frantically. "How do you want it?" he asked, while whipping out ten inches of the blackest man meat Rachel had ever seen.

The sight of his tool made Rachel's mouth water.

"Whichever way is going to give me the best orgasm, because I really need to cum badly," she said desperately. "Ok, then I got you, baby girl. Go set on the edge of that chair and her I come." He pointed to the chair in the comer of the steam room, while he continued to strip down.

No sooner than she'd reached the chair, Ted grabbed her and spun her around and pushed her backwards into the chair, dropped to his knees, pushed her thighs wide and dove head first into her creamy slit.

Rachel spread her thighs wide for him to have all the access he needed to her love box, as he tongued at her violently, sending electric waves of pleasure throughout her body. Her pussy was so hot and wet it leaked with her sticky juices from each stroke of Ted's tongue.

Ted continued his assault on her clit, until he tasted her gushing climax as Rachel nearly fell from the chair.

"Ahhh! Oohh! Eewwww!" She screamed, as she released a flood of her juices all over Ted's face. Ted jumped back quickly because of the amount of cum that continued to flow from her love box was like hot lava from a volcano.

"Holy shit, lady! I'd say you're a gusher! I've only seen something like this on a porno!" he exclaimed, while snatching her up to her feet and bending her over the chair.

"Get up there on your knees," he ordered. As she climbed up into the chair he noticed that she had a firm round backside for a white woman, and imagined that twenty years ago she probably was a head turner.

He entered Rachel from the back slowly and easily, stroking her juicy and soaking wet slit with precision. Her tight pussy felt unbelievably amazing, and Ted had to slow his stroke nearly to a halt so that he didn't erupt too early. Rachel's walls contracted around his length as she grinded backwards into him until she felt his balls slapping her ass cheeks.

"I want you all the way inside of me, Ted. Let me feel all of it," she said seductively.

He continued to stir his big black dick slowly inside of Rachel, driving her insane with pleasure.

"Spread your ass open for me and I'll go deeper for you," Ted replied watching his meat disappear in and out of her tunnel. Rachel reached back with both hands and held herself wide open for him to continue penetrating her pussy deeply.

"Go in deep! I wanna feel your balls on my clit! Do it now, dammit!" she demanded.

Ted grabbed her hips as he drove all ten inches in to the hilt and began to pound her from the back like a wild animal.

"Is this how you like it? Huh, huh? Tell me Rachel!" Ted asked aggressively, stroking her hard and fast and deep.

"Oh! Oh! Fuck yes! Yes! Fuck me good! Just like that, Ted!" she gasped.

Ted slowed his stroke, bringing it to a deeply penetrating grind, touching both sides of her walls and this made Rachel scream with delight.

"Oh! Baby! PLEASE DON'T STOP! YOU'RE A FUCKING SEX MASTER! I'M CUMMING. OH! I'M CUMMING SO HARD!" Rachel moaned as she reached another climax. Her cum gushed free once again, the force of the blast pushing past Ted's lodged tool inside of her tunnel. He felt her walls contracting around his shaft as he slowly pulled out of her, only to be blasted by cum juice that had been suppressed.

"Whoops! I'm sorry about that," she said, looking back at him after her pussy had squirted cum over his entire mid-section. Rachel collapsed on the floor, panting heavily and spent. Ted looked down at her, astonished at the amount of built up cum she'd had.

"Do you think you can stand, anymore?" he asked earnestly.

"Give me a second, and let me catch my breath first," she gasped.

"Fuck that! The next round belongs to me! Turn your ass over and lay flat on your stomach," he said helping her to turn over.

Once on her stomach he straddled her from behind, and spread her open and spit on his middle finger before inserting it in her asshole.

"Oouucchh! Oh, please, be gentle with me back there. I haven't had it in my ass for a very long time," she pleaded.

"I thought you came here for some dick?! Well, don't get scared now, Rachel" he said, removing his finger and replacing it with the tip of his dick.

"Listen, mutherfucker! I'm not afraid of anything! Especially not any dick! I can take all you got with ease! Try me and see mutherfucker!" she said smugly, now arching her back up toward him to meet his thrust.

Ted parted her ass roughly and drove his dick down into her forcefully until he was balls deep, and began to pound away at her tight walls, as she belted out racial slurs at him:

"OH YES! THAT'S RIGHT YOU FUCKING NIGGER! FUCK THIS WHITE ASS WITH YOUR BIG BLACK COCK! YOU BIG BLACK MUTHERFUCKER! HARDER! HARDER! BANG MY ASS OUT! YES! YES!"

Ted was slamming into her asshole with all his might, drilling her relentlessly like an animal, as Rachel continued to buck wildly back into his thrust.

"TAKE ALL THIS DICK YOU WHITE BITCH!" he replied as his balls began to swell. He reached under her waist and hoisted her up to her feet, and then into mid-air with his pole lodged inside of her ass, while he continued to bang her tight ass now standing up.

"Yea White BITCH! I DON'T HEAR YOU TALKING SHIT NOW, DO I?! I GOT THAT WHITE ASS NOW!" Ted said huskily into her ear as she was visibly in pain from the pounding he was giving her ass from a different position.

He finally released her, lifting her up off his pole and Rachel immediately dropped to the floor and curled into the fetal position.

"Hell Naw, Bitch! YOU DON'T GET OFF THAT EASY! GET OVER HERE AND CLEAN UP YOUR MESS" he commanded, as he snatched her by her blonde hair and shoved his dick into her mouth.

Rachel used both hands to stroke his shaft while sucking the first big black dick she'd ever tasted.

"Look at me while you suck my dick, white bitch! The jokes on you now ain't it? Are you still having fun?" he asked, while pumping her face, She nodded her approval and continued to slurp away, bringing him to an explosive climax.

"Oh yea! I'm cumming for you now! It's my turn and you'd better swallow every drop! Don't you spill a drop, white bitch!" Ted groaned as he closed his eyes and released his thick and creamy load of cum into her warm mouth. His juice continued to spout until Rachel could swallow no more, and she turned his assault weapon towards her breasts, soaking her nipples with his excess juice.

"Holy smokes! Now that's what I'd call amazing!" Rachel exclaimed, now winded and panting heavily and smiling. Ted stared down at her, his erection not completely deflated.

"I'll take my money now. I believe I've earned it," he said, smiling back at her.

"Oh honey, believe me, you definitely earned your money. Every dime of it plus some! You're fucking awesome!" she exclaimed, reaching for her clothes.

It was just past midnight and the two were seated at his desk again.

"Ok, sweetheart, I want you to charge me forty-five hundred. I'll be back to collect my other session in the near future so I want to be paid up," she said, handing him her husband's credit card.

"That's definitely fine by me, Rachel. I really appreciate you looking out for me. Here's my card and you're welcome to call me anytime, and I do mean *anytime*."

Rachel tip-toed into her bedroom, and found her husband fast asleep with the TV still on. She stripped down and slid under the blanket trying not to wake him.

"Honey, you must've had a hellava workout tonight," he mumbled, slightly waking up.

"Oh hey, honey. Yes, I certainly did as a matter of fact and it felt amazing. Thank you, Dan, for supporting me with this," she whispered.

"Anything for you, honey. You know I'd do anything to see you happy," he replied, sliding over to her side of the bed. "Wow, Rachel, you're still hot and you feel kind of shaky," he continued as he stroked her arms.

"Oh trust me, Danny, if I'm going to pay for a personal trainer, I'm damn sure gonna get my money's worth," she replied.

"That's my girl. Now let's get some sleep, shall we?" he said, sliding back over to his side of the bed.

"Yea, I'm exhausted. Goodnight, Dan," she said, barely audible under the covers. Rachel could still taste Ted in her mouth and smell his scent.

"Sweet dreams, honey," she mumbled and closed her eyes.

NIGHT TRAIN

~~~~~~

"Yo, I'm headed home dog! I gotta be up early in the a.m.to punch in," Quan said to his homie, Jermaine, as they walked down 115th street. They'd been hanging out at a local strip club, smoking blunts, drinking tequila and getting lap dances.

Quan had recently been promoted to manager at his factory job, which meant that he'd have to end his late night out with his homie in order to wake up and be on time the following morning.

"Come on man, the party's just getting started. I wanted to head over to the Pink Lace and check out the new talent I heard is up in there!!" Jermaine replied.

"Well, help yourself and go ahead and keep the party going then, but this brother right here gots to earn a living, ya dig. Peace out for now, dog. Be safe. And remember, if you happen to get stopped by the police for being black, put your hands up!" Quan said as they laughed, gave each other daps and parted ways for the night.

Quan briefly thought about walking home because the night air was sobering him up, but as he approached the subway entrance he quickly changed his mind.

Quan went down the steps leading to the subway station and sat on a bench waiting for his L to pull up. It was empty in the station, which wasn't unusual at this hour in the morning. Quan got up and went to the restroom and, after relieving himself, washed his hands and went back out to the bench. He had just sat down when he heard his train coming. He stood up as it pulled into the station and finally came to a stop.

Quan waited for the doors to slide open, then he stepped on and was about to make his way to the last car, but before the doors could close all the way he heard a female voice call out, "Hold the doors please!"

Quan turned and saw a white woman running towards the train. He caught the door and pushed it back open, and the woman got on.

"Hey, whew!" she said, catching her breath. "Thanks. These fucking things come early, come late –"

"Yeah, I know, right," Quan said, turning to head to the back of the train.

He had to go through two cars, which both were occupied with just a sprinkle of people, but the third and last car was empty. Quan sat in the last seat and saw that the white chick had followed him.

She was wearing black combat boots with heels, black fishnet stockings, a short black skirt, a black short sleeve, half shirt that said: *What the HELL is heaven?!* on the front, black gloves with the fingers cut out, and a black collar with clear spikes on it. She wore black lipstick, black eye liner, and her hair was short and black with green highlights. She even was wearing black reading glasses.

Quan quickly decided that this pink toe was way out there.

"Hey, thanks again for holding the door. My name's Rabbit," she said, holding out her hand for him to shake.

"I'm Quan, and it's always a pleasure helping a beautiful woman, ma," Quan said.

"Dude," Rabbit said, laughing. "You are soooo full of fucking shit, right now! I mean, I do have a fucking TV. I know what type of women black guys like, but thanks for the compliment anyway."

She lit a cigarette, then offered Quan one, but he pulled out his own.

"So, what type of girl do I like then?" Quan asked, smiling as she reached over and lit his cigarette.

"Come on, dude, are you serious right now? I mean, you know when it's a black chick you people," Rabbit started to say, and then busted out in laughter at the expression on Quan's face when she'd said 'you people.'

"Dude," she said, after she had stopped laughing. "That was a joke. But anyway, when it's a black chick, y'all like them with big ole tits and a big, huge ass and all that. If it's a white chick, then you want her to be all prissy and blonde with nice tits, though it probably wouldn't hurt if she had a little booty too, huh?"

She smiled, pushed her glasses up, then took another puff of her cigarette. "And as you can see, I don't have any of that".

"Actually, I can't see," Quan said, turning towards her, putting his arm across the head rest of her seat. "I can't see what you have or don't have cause you ain't showed me nothing ma."

"Oh, yeah. You're good. That's another thing that I learned. Well, actually, I only heard this," Rabbit said, flicking the ash of her cigarette onto the floor.

"And what'd you hear?" Quan asked her, scooting a little closer to her.

"Oh, just that you guys are smooth talkers," she said, leaning her head back on his arm for a second, then lifting it off. She hit the cigarette again, said, "And I heard some more shit too, but —"

Quan couldn't help but let his eyes roam up Rabbit's fishnet wrapped legs. He looked at her flat stomach that was exposed by the half shirt she was wearing. He noticed that she had a black, horseshoe shaped navel ring.

"Quan. Dude, I'm up here," she said, smiling again.

"I'm sorry. I just couldn't help it," Quan said, smiling back at her. "So what's the other shit you heard?" he asked.

"Well, dude, I mean, you know, well, shit! I heard that you guys are like, really packing," she said, looking him square in the eyes.

The train's lights blinked off in the car they were sitting in, then came back on.

"How old are you, Rabbit?" Quan asked.

"Don't worry, man. I'm not a minor. I'm nineteen. Why?" Rabbit said.

"Wanna find out for yourself, ma?" Quan asked her. And before she could answer, he took her hand and put it on the bulge forming in his jeans.

"Dude! That is NOT what I think it is," Rabbit said, looking at the growing lump her hand was covering. She squeezed it, then turned all the way towards him, putting her other hand in his lap.

"You know how to find out," Quan said, and leaned back in his seat.

Rabbit decided that this would probably be her only, or at least, her best chance at seeing some black meat in real life so she went for it. She undid his belt, unbuttoned and unzipped his jeans, looked over her shoulder to make sure they still had the car to themselves, and pulled his pants down to mid-thigh.

"HOLY SHIT!" she said, pulling his dick out.

She got out of her seat and got on her knees in front of him. Rabbit looked at Quan, and then pushed his dick up against his stomach and started sucking his balls.

"Oh, shit!" Quan moaned, letting his head fall back.

Rabbit sucked Quan's left nut, then moved to his right one. Once she had gave each of his balls some attention she wrapped her hand around his ball sack, making both his nuts gather in the same spot, then she sucked them both at the same time.

"Awww, yeah ma, suck on them balls just like that," Quan said, looking down at her again.

"You like that, huh? You like how I just sucked your balls," Rabbit asked, then licked a trail from Quan's balls to the head of his dick, and then she grabbed the base of his shaft. Rabbit sucked on his dick head once, twice, then on the third time she went down on his throbbing pole until her lips touched her fist.

"Quan's toes curled up in his Jordan's as he reached down, putting his hands on the back of her head. Rabbit stayed in that position for a few seconds, then came up real slow. When she got to the last two inches of his dick she opened her mouth wide and stuck her tongue out letting his dick slide slowly off of it.

"Dude, this is the first time I ever sucked a black cock," Rabbit said, with his dick resting against her cheek.

"Is that right? Well, shit ma, you're doing an excellent job for a first timer," Quan replied, bending and reaching down to slip a hand under her skirt and into her panties from the back. His fingers slid over her asshole, then into her hot, tight snatch.

"Mmmmm. Ungh, ungh. Nope," Rabbit said, after letting him finger her dripping hole a couple of times. "You gotta sit back so I can finish what I started."

Rabbit pushed him back. Quan got comfortable and let her do her thing.

Rabbit took her hand off his rigid fuck stick, then started sucking it without using her hands. Her head was bobbing up and down and saliva was running from her mouth down his shaft to his balls. The slurping noises she was making was adding to the sensations and driving Quan closer to that point. Rabbit went all the way down his shaft and Quan felt his balls tighten up.

"Awwww shit! Here it comes," Quan said, with a clenched jaw, bracing himself for what felt like one of the biggest nuts he'd ever busted.

Rabbit pulled her mouth off his throbbing member and started stroking it with her hand and flicking her tongue on the head. "Come on, motherfucker, shoot that cum on my fucking face! Come on. Give it to me!" Rabbit said, jacking his dick furiously.

Quan gave it to her just like she asked. He erupted like a shaken champagne bottle, soaking Rabbit's face with his thick hot cream. As his cum subsided, he looked down at her jizz covered face, thinking that he'd be taking the night train every night.

ROOKIE NOOKIE

Ariette's first week at her new job had been a piece of cake!

"Ha! I can't believe I'm actually getting paid to do this! Hell, I'd show up for free if I had to!" she'd told her sister, Julia, who'd been responsible for helping her land the job at the federal correctional institution in California.

Ariette had turned wild child during her first year of junior college, and she'd partied her way out of college and back into her parent's home broke and jobless, failing miserably at life on her own.

Julia stepped in to help Ariette get back on track, and offered her a temporary place to stay. Her husband David, who was a correctional officer at the prison in town, put in a word of recommendation for Ariette, who desperately needed employment.

Any reservations Julia had had about her baby sister working in a prison, David quickly put to rest, letting her know that all the prisoners Ariette would encounter would be non-violent drug dealers, who were not any threat to her safety.

"All she'll have to do is show up on time, count the inmates, and collect a paycheck. That's it." David had said.

Neither Julia nor David had been aware that Ariette had been dating young black men while in junior college and, frankly, couldn't get enough of them. She definitely had jungle fever.

Ariette arrived early for her evening shift at the prison. She double checked her platinum blonde hair and make-up in her rearview mirror, making sure everything was in place before heading inside.

Once being buzzed in through the security clearance station, she checked in the guards shack, where she retrieved her guard's belt that came equipped with handcuffs, pepper spray, walkie-talkie, and keys. She read the bulletin board, searching for her name to see where she'd been assigned to work for her shift. She spotted her name assigned to the medical department and quickly became excited, having worked there her first week on the job and meeting Derrick, who was an inmate orderly for the medical staff. Derrick was a clean-cut, forty-two year old brother. He stood six foot even, light complexion, with a bald head and muscular build.

He carried himself with an attitude of complete confidence and positivity, and after serving eleven years of a twenty year sentence, he'd recently been granted a time reduction that was giving him his freedom back within the next sixty days.

Ariette was looking forward to continuing their last conversation where they'd left off, and had also left her horny as well. Ariette found herself very attracted to Derrick, who hadn't been with a woman in many years, and had some anxiety about how his first encounter would be.

"Oh, come on now! You mean to tell me that you've never even once eaten pussy! Ha! That's just so totally hard for me to believe!" Ariette exclaimed.

Derrick laughed and was amused.

"Nope! Sorry youngsta. That just wasn't the *in thing* back when I was out. People just didn't go around putting their mouths on people so freely, and if they did then they were secretive about that sort of thing. Hell, and the women weren't all that outspoken about sucking dick either for that matter! It was all kinda hush-hush," Derrick responded.

"Well I'm proud of my abilities, and it's no secret that I absolutely love sucking dick, and I'm not ashamed to admit it either," She smirked.

"O'yea, is that right? Well, who is it that says your abilities are what you assume they may be? I mean, your boyfriend just may not want to hurt your feelings, or he may not have much to compare your abilities to, with you being so young and all," he teased her.

"I'll beg your pardon! I'll have you know that every man I've been with so far hasn't had any complaints! And for the record, I don't have, or want any boyfriend. I'm single and available to mingle, thank you very much. Now you on the other hand need to be worrying about yourself, mister *I ain't never ate no pussy* before, because you're gonna have a hard time keeping a good woman if you don't know what you're doing when you get out there," she replied.

"Well how do you suggest that I'm going to learn if I've never been taught?" Derrick replied, giving her a wicked grin.

"Tell you what. Meet me in the nurses break room after their shift is over and I'll be happy to give you your first lesson, and that's a direct order. I wouldn't want you to go out into society not having the tools you'll need ya know," she said jokingly.

Derrick's heart skipped a beat as he thought about officer Ariette's offer. His manhood immediately reacted and the shift change couldn't come fast enough!

Toying with Ariette had been fun for Derrick, and after she'd taken the bait, it was like taking candy from a baby. After all, he'd been working in the medical department for years and had his share of the lonely and horny C.N.A.'s and nurses after hours.

Ariette came into the nurses break room as promised once she'd walked the last nurse out of the medical department and was sure that she and Derrick were absolutely alone. Derrick was waiting for her, sprawled across a futon with his hands folded behind his head watching the small television in the break room.

"Hey you, are you ready for your lesson?" Ariette asked, with a quick smile, sliding down next to him on the worn out futon and rubbing her hands across his broad chest.

Derrick unfolded his hands behind his head and wrapped her in his arms, pulling her on top of him. His manhood throbbed against her as she straddled him and they were now face to face.

"You can feel just how ready I am for you," he said, nudging her with his erection.

"We have about twenty minutes before I have to be back in my cell, so we gotta get moving," Derrick continued, now kissing her neck and unbuttoning her shirt.

Ariette's breathing grew heavy as Derricks lips went from her neck down to her chest. His hands stroked and caressed her body with a lust and eagerness that she hadn't felt before.

Once her shirt was unbuttoned and her breasts were exposed to him, he took each of her breasts into his strong hands, holding them firmly as he sucked at her nipples and pulled them into his mouth.

She ran her hands along his broad shoulders and back and began to moan, the warmth of his tongue sending electric waves of ecstasy through her body.

In one swift motion, he'd rolled over on top of her, her legs wrapped around his waist. He continued kissing her, working his way down from her breast, to her stomach, and then further down. She eagerly unbuttoned her guard's belt, allowing it to fall to the floor with a loud thud.

Derrick unfastened her pants quickly as she helped him.

Once out of her pants, Ariette laid on her back as Derrick positioned himself between her thighs, again looking her directly into her eyes.

"Are you ready, coach?" he smirked, as he went down on her, kissing her first between her warm thighs, allowing his tongue to linger.

Ariette spread her thighs wide, now panting and breathing heavily. She slid her black thong to the side for him, exposing her completely bare and smooth pussy.

"Come up here, Derrick. Start right here." She pointed to the top of her slit.

Derrick worked his way up to where she'd instructed, slowly placing his mouth on her love button while he held her thighs wide. She grabbed the back of his head and pulled him onto her, screaming and quivering.

"OHH, YEA! Work your tongue right there over and over again. YEA, YEA, just like that. OHH, Don't stop!" she continued moaning.

Derrick stroked her clit with his tongue repeatedly until he felt her thighs tighten around his shoulders. Ariette began to shudder.

"Oh, oh, FUCK! I'M CUMMING! OHH! YEA, YEA!" she panted.

Derrick licked her wetness until she stilled and finally relaxed.

"How'd I do for my first lesson?" he asked, looking up at her flushed face.

"Amazing! That's the best I've ever had! It's almost hard to believe that you've never done that before! I'd say you're a natural!" she exclaimed, still winded from the orgasm that had ripped through her body.

Derrick released her and stood, unbuckling his khaki pants.

"Now it's your turn to show me," he said, freeing his nine-inch tool for her to demonstrate with.

Ariette immediately rose from her back to take him into her warm and welcoming mouth.

"Oh, it's my pleasure," she said, grabbing him by his shaft and licking at his tip before shoving his big thick rod into her throat.

Derrick stood and watched as she sucked and slurped, eager to make him bust.

"Suck on my balls, too, baby," he said, removing his dick from her mouth and holding his ball sack for her to suck..

"UMMMM," she moaned, while taking each of his balls into her mouth greedily, while she stroked his dick at the same time. "I wanna taste your cum, baby. Give it to me," she said putting his dick back into her mouth and deep throating him repeatedly.

Derrick was on the brink of cumming down her throat when Ariette abruptly stopped and stood up.

"Put it in me! I wanna feel that beautiful black cock inside of my tight pussy!" Ariette panted, climbing onto her knees on the futon. Derrick moved in behind her, grabbing her ass and sinking himself balls deep into her hot split. He stroked her deep, long and hard rapidly.

"Oh, shit! This pussy is tight," he exclaimed, feeling himself on the brink of releasing an explosion into Ariette.

"Derrick! I'm gonna cum! Oh, baby, I'm gonna cum all over your big black cock! Smack my ass and pull my hair!" she screamed as her inner walls tightened around his tool, preparing for an orgasm.

Derrick smacked her ass firmly until her backside was cherry red. Then he grabbed a handful of her platinum blonde hair and pulled it tightly as she exploded.

"Holy shit! I'm cumming so fucking hard! Yes, yes, yes!" she moaned.

At this, Derrick's balls swelled and he had to release his load at once. He eased from inside her honey pot quickly, and Ariette spun around and dropped to her knees.

"Come and get what you want," he said, driving his sticky cock deeply into her wanting mouth. Ariette sucked him violently, until she felt his eruption, swallowing his juices as he blasted her throat.

"Oh, oh! Fuck, that was good!" he said as he grunted, his knees wobbly and nearly buckling.

"So, do you still doubt my abilities, Derrick?" Ariette asked, looking up at him with a wicked smile.

"You're definitely a hellava rookie, Ariette," he said, as he pulled his pants up, and began to straighten out his collar.

BABYSITTER
NEEDED

~~~~~~

I was looking through the morning paper that day when I came across the ad: BABYSITTER NEEDED? I GOT YOU!

There wasn't anything special or cryptic about the ad that made me decide to pick up my cell phone and dial the number that was listed. Truth be told, I was simply going to need a babysitter. I wasn't a single father or anything, it's just that my sister and her husband were on a vacation and I was their designated babysitter, not to mention a free one at that.

Now, before you judge me and deem me to be a no good uncle, that would pass off the responsibility of watching his four-year old niece to some stranger just to enjoy himself with some random chick, understand that my sister and her husband were told in advance about my upcoming date and so, had advised me to hire a babysitter for that day. They had even left me with the money to pay this future baby sitter, so all parties were in agreement and everything was cool.

I dialed the number and then lit the blunt I'd rolled before going onto the deck of my house.

"Hello," a female voice said. She sounded like a young white girl.

"Uh yes, I," I tried to say, coughing from the weed, which was some good lemon kush. After I regained my composure, I said, "Excuse me. I'm calling about the ad in the newspaper for a babysitter."

"Awesome! Hey, my name is Cindy. I'm eighteen and everyone loves me! Even animals. Especially kids. Yeah, kids say I rock! Oh, sorry, how can I help you?" Cindy asked.

Yep, definitely a white girl I said to myself.

"Well, Cindy I'm going to be in need of a babysitter for Thursday, but I'd like to meet in person just to make sure you're not a crazy lil girl who likes to eat kids," I said, starting to laugh, though the laugh instead had turned into a cough.

I put the blunt out in the ashtray, then went to sit on a lounge chair. Cindy herself laughed, then said, "Dude. For one, I'm like, far from a little girl, and for two, I need to make sure that you are not some type of creepo who preys on beautiful young women like myself."

I couldn't help but laugh. It wasn't that what she had said was all that funny; it was because she sounded like the *epitome* of a suburban white girl, as if she belonged on a T V show.

"What time'll be cool for you, Cindy-the-not-a-lil-girl? Because I'm free now," I said, lighting the blunt again and looking at my reflection in the patio's sliding doors.

I could hear her talking to someone else for a minute and then she said, "Well, since I'm out and about right now, I guess I could come by. But, I'm bringing my friend and my Tazer with me, and by the way, if you call me a little girl again and I'll taze you in your balls. Then you can explain that to your wife." She replied, laughing.

"I'll beg your pardon? I don't have to explain myself to anybody because I'm single," I told her, thinking why did I add the single part. I continued to set on my patio, stunned at the conversation I was having.

"That's what they all say. Anyway, what's the address?"

"Twenty-one-oh-nine Arrowhead. There'll be a white Charger in the driveway. You know how to get here?"

"Uh, yeah. Is ten minutes cool?"

"Yeah, that'll work. Look though, when you get here come up on the back patio," I said, getting up to go check on my niece who had been watching a cartoon movie on the flat screen in the guest bedroom.

She was still in the same place. She asked could she have some juice and I told her yes. I went and got it for her and then left her to her entertainment. I went upstairs and poured a healthy glass of Remy and then went back out on the patio and lit a cigarette. I had just taken my third sip, when a cute, but skinny, white girl peeked around the side of the house.

When she saw me standing there she came around, cautiously with a nervous smile on her face. She was without a doubt a pretty ass white girl. She was wearing a pink, woman's wife beater, very small, white denim shorts, and a pair of pink and white Jordans. Her hair was done in one long braid that hung down her back. She reminded me of a Miley Cyrus.

"You must be, Cindy. I'm Jaron Williams. I'm the one who called you. We can have a seat out here or we can go inside," I said, standing up and extending my hand for her to shake.

"Hey, Mr. Williams. Um, nice to meet you. I'm cool out here. Is this your house? I mean, you live here by yourself!" she asked, looking around at the spacious backyard, then inside the house through the patio doors.

After getting her eyeful of the house she turned towards me and took the seat opposite of where I'd been sitting.

"Yeah, it's just me. Though I have my niece here for a week and that's the reason I called," I said, taking the blunt I'd been smoking out the ashtray. "You don't mind if I smoke?" I asked.

"Not as long as I can smoke with you," Cindy said, smiling.

"I don't smoke with kids. No, no, no. You won't have me sitting in jail," I said.

"I don't see any kids around. Just a woman and an old man," she smiled, reaching for the blunt. "Here let me light that for you, grandpa."

I laughed and let her take the blunt. I stood up to go refill my glass.

"Would you like something to drink? I got juices, sodas, and I think some Kool-Aid," I asked her.

"Yeah, I want some of what you got. I mean what you're drinking now," she said, hitting the blunt and then coughing a little.

I can't lie. Well, I can but I won't. My dick detected a hidden meaning in what she had said. I told myself that I was tripping from the Remy and the weed and wasn't even about to go down that road with this young girl. *White girl* at that. I also decided not to give her any alcohol, even though I'd just let her smoke with me.

I just got her a glass of strawberry soda, then went and checked on my niece, who asked me for some pop tarts and said she wanted to Watch Happy Feet-2, so I put the movie on, got her the pop tarts, then left her to her movie and snacks.

When I stepped back out on the patio, Cindy was leaning back on her elbows on the futon with just her bra, panties, and Jordans on. She had her legs hanging over the sides of the futon, wide open. Good thing that I had a privacy fence.

"Don't freak out, but this is the perfect place for some sun," she said, handing me the blunt and taking the soda.

I took a big sip of my drink then sat it on the table and hit the blunt. As bad as I wanted to, I told myself I would have to pass on the little marshmallow. I don't know why, but I went and stood on her side of the table instead of sitting in the chair on the opposite side.

I leaned against the rail and hit the blunt again. *Hard.* I passed her the blunt and she passed me my drink after she had taken a good drink out of. Fuck it then, I said to myself. I turned towards her and she turned over on her stomach showing her little white ass cheeks and the G-string that was slid in between them.

"I want to hit this, now," she said, reaching out and grabbing my dick. It jumped in her hand, "Damn!" she said, feeling it.

"Yeah, that's a grown man dick there. You wouldn't know what to do with that," I said, finishing the rest of my drink.

Cindy looked up at me and smiled, then sat up on the edge of the futon, and started to unzip my pants. That done, she pulled them down, then without a second's hesitation she started to lick me from my balls to the head. The bottom, the sides, the top. Then she sucked my dick pretty good and what she lacked in skill she made up for with a lot of enthusiasm and porno type sound effects.

I picked her up, pulled her bra down under her titties and sucked and nibbled on her nipples, licking around her areolas. Then I sat her on the rail of the patio, pulled her panties to the side and proceeded to fuck her until she squirted. When it was over I ended up having to help her to her car because she said her legs wouldn't stop shaking.

Oh, and we definitely set the day and time for her to come babysit my niece, lol.

BREAK TIME

~~~~~~

Joanna had been working at the clothing factory for five years. She'd moved up and become a shift supervisor, and it was her responsibility to orientate the newly hired employees. Her last group of newly hired employees was an interesting group, especially the twenty six year old chocolate brother that stood out from the group, named Michael.

Michael had transferred in from an out of state location, and knew the how it worked in the company's factory right off the bat. His deep brown skin and lean frame had immediately attracted Joanna, and his smile and flirtatious demeanor let her know that the two were soon to enjoy one another's company. Just how soon was the million dollar question that was answered unexpectedly.

It was 9:45am, when the announcement boomed through the factory's intercom.

"LADIES AND GENTLEMEN, IT IS NOW 9:45 A.M., AND IT IS OFFICIALLY BREAK TIME. WORK CALL WILL RESUME AT 10:30 A.M. ENJOY YOUR LUNCH BREAK."

As the workers crowded their way to the front doors to leave, heading to the parking lot with cigarettes hanging from their lips, Joanna spotted Michael near the locker room texting on his cell phone.

"Hey you, you aren't going out for lunch?" Joanna asked, as she approached him smiling.

"Naw, I'm hanging back. I brought my lunch in with me today. "Why, what are your plans for lunch?" Michael asked, returning her smile.

Joanna moved in close to Michael, until they were standing nose to nose.

"I think I might like something different."

"Like what?" asked Michael.

Joanna placed her hand on his crotch and rubbed.

The next thing she knew, she was on her knees sucking his huge, glorious cock for all she was worth.

She felt his hands tighten on the back of her head, and suddenly her mouth was filled with his thick cream as he grunted with pleasure.

"UMNNN, AHHH!" he continued, as he released. Joanna sucked and swallowed all that he had to spill, nursing him in her mouth, feeling his hardness return.

She stood and quickly took off her denim jeans.

"Sit down so I can I ride that cock for you," she exclaimed hurriedly.

Michael complied just as quickly. He held his pole straight up for her to slide down on, and once she was straddled in, Joanna began to cream instantly.

"AHH FUCK!" she screamed out in passion, riding his dick hard and fast.

Michael kissed her neck in a fury, while palming her backside firmly as she rode him steadily.

"I'm gonna cum, Michael! OHH Ahh! I'm gonna cum!" she continued as she bucked her hips and her walls contracted. Michael began to thrust upward into her wet snatch, driving his manhood deeper into her, and held her in place as she orgasmed on his lap.

"AHAH! Michael! Michael! I'm cumming!" Joanna exploded from deep inside, going limp as Michael continued to thrust into her fuck hole. Joanna's release caused Michael to let go as well, and soon Joanna felt him swell inside of her tightness and flood her with the warmth of his second orgasm. He pumped his juice into her until there wasn't a drop left.

The two looked at each other, spent and breathing heavily.

"We gotta do lunch more often, Michael," she smiled.

CLEAN UP ON AISLE #5

Linda was so happy that she didn't have to go into work today that she woke up smiling.

She had her whole day planned. She was going grocery shopping first, then go to the Legends Mall to do a little light shopping, probably get herself a new purse and maybe even a few new sun dresses, and then treat herself to dinner in town – Outback Steak House or Olive Garden.

Today was her forty-second birthday and she was going to enjoy it. After showering, dressing and eating a little breakfast, she called her best friend Cheryl.

"Hello, Lin. Happy birthday! How does it feel to be on the opposite side of young?" Cheryl said, laughing.

"Well, Cherry, now that I think about it...yeah, I'd have to say that now I know how you've been feeling for the last decade," Linda replied, and laughed.

Cheryl was fifty-one, but she looked twenty years younger than that. There were times though when she acted as if she was even younger than she looked.

"Screw you, Lin. Now that I think about it, I might just have to because, Lord knows, no one else is, "Cheryl said good-naturedly.

"Oh hush, Cherry. Everyone doesn't have the time to be an enthusiastic nympho like you. For one you're of the esteemed upper class while I, on the other hand, have to work for a living, though not today. So you're going to spend the day with your best friend on her birthday and her only day off from work this week, and you are going to enjoy it," Linda said, deciding to wear a light strapless dress, no bra or panties since it was supposed to be somewhere in the high nineties and she would be out most of the day.

"You know what Cherry? I'm gonna do something daring today," Linda said, looking at her body in the mirror on her closet door.

She wasn't disappointed with her body, though she was far from a sex kitten, as Cheryl liked to put it. She wasn't one of those Curves Magazine looking women, either. But, on the whole she was sure she could still turn a head or two if she applied herself.

"And what might this daring thing be? Don't tell me you're going to wear a mini skirt and some come fuck me heels," Cheryl said, laughing.

"Ha, ha. Funny, but no. I'm not going to wear a bra or panties today. And I'm going to wear a strapless, white garden dress, but don't worry, it doesn't have flowers on it or anything. When the sun or the right light hits it, though, you can see right through it, but you have to do the same," Linda told her.

"Lin honey, there are seven days in a week, and unless things have changed since you and I have been on the phone, out of those seven days I may wear panties on one or two of them," Cheryl said, as if it was the most normal thing in the world to do. "But of course, since you are my best friend, I'd agree to go around town completely naked, if that's what you wanted to do for your birthday."

They talked for a little while longer, then Linda told her she wanted to get her grocery shopping done first, while it wasn't that hot.

"Alright. We'll take my Range Rover because it's bigger than your little Mercury, and the air conditioning works. I'll be there in say, forty five. How's that?" Cheryl asked.

"That's fine. I'll be ready. See you then, bye," Linda said, and hung up.

"Oh my," Cheryl said, nudging Linda's shoulder to get her attention. "Would you look at that hunk of a man over there! The black guy over there stocking the shelves in aisle four I think it is. Yeah, it's four. "

"Oooh, he is handsome. Cherry, have you...have you ever had one?" she asked, lowering her voice and looking around as if they were talking about a plot to rob the grocery store.

"Had one what?" Cheryl asked, scanning the store for more male eye candy.

"You know. Have you ever had a black man before?" Linda asked, smiling.

Cheryl stopped and looked at her friend, then started walking again until she found an empty aisle.

She directed Linda into the aisle, then turned to her, "Are you serious? Well, I don't even need to ask that, I can see it written all on your face," Cheryl said, smiling, eyes sparkling.

"What? What're you talking about?" Linda interrupted, but then Cheryl cut her off.

"You, my dear girl, want to have sex with a black guy! I can see it in your eyes. And no, I haven't had one but this would be the perfect time. I'm in need of a good banging. Hell, and if I am, Lord knows you're probably ready to fucking explode!" Cheryl said, looking like a hungry cougar at that moment. She started walking, taking Linda's hand and pulling her along.

"I have to say this, it'll be the perfect birthday present for you, and a much needed tuning up for me," Cheryl continued.

Linda was shocked by Cheryl's suggestion, but also to her very own disbelief she was excited at the thought of some good 'birthday sex.'

She had just started to play out a fantasy in her mind, when Cheryl said, "Oh, this is just perfect! He's still there and we have the aisle to ourselves. Now look, Lin, just let me do the talking and follow my lead."

Cheryl put on her turtle shell BCBG sunglasses, ran her fingers through her hair, then glanced at the black guy at the opposite end of the aisle. He had his back to them bent over opening a box with a box cutter.

Cheryl looked at Linda, then took a jar of tomato sauce off the shelf to her left, held it high, then dropped it. The jar hit the tile floor with a crash and they both flinched reflexively.

Tony, who had been working at Master Mart for only a week was thinking to himself that he couldn't wait to get off work, go home and take a shower, then have a drink and smoke a blunt when he heard the sound of glass shattering behind him.

Here we go. Probably some fucking kids making my job harder, he thought. Tony turned around putting on his best smile which wasn't at all hard, when he saw the two snow bunnies standing there. Well, snow cougars was more like it, since they were older women.

"Oh, look at the mess I've made. I'm so sorry! It just slipped right out of my hands," Cheryl said, as the young man came over.

She hiked her skirt up to her knees not failing to notice that Linda had done the same, then squatted down to pick up pieces of the glass.

She knew that as soon as the guy got down to pick-up the glass he would undoubtedly see their pink pussies. And she didn't know about Linda, but hers was sure as hell wet just from the thought of this fine, young, black stallion.

Tony saw the women trying to pick up the glass and didn't want them to accidently cut themselves, so he dropped down on one knee.

"Don't worry about it ladies. I'll take care of this. I'd hate it if you two beautiful women got cut. I mean I —" Tony started to say, as he started picking up the glass, but then he looked up and forgot what he had been saying when he saw the women's pussy lips peeking at him. Tony damn near cut himself when he saw that. Neither one of the two white ladies had panties on!

"I got to be dreaming," Tony thought.

"Cheryl watched Tony look under her dress, then under Linda's. She glanced at Linda, who was breathing hard and had a red flush to her face.

"Um, Tony. You might want to pay attention to what you're doing before you cut yourself. Because if you pass out, then Linda and I will have to give you mouth to mouth," Cheryl said, reaching out and grabbing Tony's throbbing bulge that was clearly visible.

"Or maybe we can go somewhere and put our mouths on something else of yours," Linda said in a husky voice that wasn't familiar to her own ears.

Tony couldn't believe it. At first his mind made the assessment that the situation was just a test from the manager, since he was still on his probation period. He almost laughed out loud at that thought.

If this is a test, well then, fuck it, I'm going to fail this one, he thought as he stood up and took both ladies hands and helped them to their feet.

"Yeah, as a matter of fact there is a place. Ladies, follow me. Tony replied, leading the way.

"My name is Cheryl, by the way, and this is Linda."

"I'm Tony, and it's my pleasure to meet you two," Tony replied, standing in an aisle crammed by pallets stocked with cases of different items. Tony had used this place to smoke cigarettes at times, so he knew that they would be alright back here and away from prying eyes.

"Soooo, today is Linda's birthday and she wants, or actually, we both want some black cock for her birthday. And quite frankly, Tony you're going to be the young man to give it to us," Cheryl told him.

Tony pulled a card board pallet cover from a stack by the wall and sat it on a stack of unused pallets.

"Get up there on your hands and knees, both of y'all," he said, untucking his Master Mart shirt from out of his jeans and pulling it off.

"First, let us suck that black cock of yours," Cheryl said, pulling the top of her dress down, and freeing her milky white breasts. Tony didn't have a problem with that request, but upon seeing Cheryl's luscious globes with their brown nipples sticking out, he had to have a taste of them first.

He took Cheryl's breasts in his hands and squeezed on them a little, pinching her nipples.

"Mmmm, yes," Cheryl said, reaching over and pulling the top of Linda's dress down also.

Tony went to sucking and licking on Cheryl's breasts and nipples before switching to Linda's, which were a little smaller with pink nipples and puffy areolas.

While Tony attacked Linda's breasts, Cheryl stepped behind her friend, moving the hair from Linda's neck and whispered in her ear, "Happy birthday, Lin!" Then Cheryl started to lick and kiss Linda's neck to a shiver.

Tony reached down and lifted Linda's dress and started to rub her clit.

"Oh, oh, yes, oh!" Linda moaned. Tony didn't want to waste another second, so he stepped back and undid his pants, pulling them down along with his boxers. When Cheryl and Linda saw his black snake jump out their eyes became as big as quarters!

"Oh, it's beautiful!" Cheryl said, going to her knees immediately and wrapping her hand around his long and hard black cock.

"Jesus! It looks like a baseball bat!" Linda said, squatting down next to her friend.

"Okay birthday girl, let's see if you can blow out the candle stick," Tony said, and then burst out laughing at how much that sounded like a line in a porno movie.

Cheryl and Linda both started laughing with him, which helped with Linda's nerves.

Still gripping Tony's rod, Cheryl pointed it towards her friend, "Here, Lin, blow," she said, smiling.

Linda didn't hesitate as she gobbled up Tony's throbbing manhood like a born pro. The taste of his pre cum on her tongue turned her on even more. Cheryl pulled his man meat from Linda's mouth and started sucking and licking it, so Linda moved to Tony's balls.

"Ooh! Fuck, yeah! Work that dick and them balls. Just like that. Ahhh, shit yes!" Tony growled, then stepped back, pulling his dick from the two horny white women's mouths.

"Okay ladies, Get y'all asses up there face down, and ass up," he said, stroking his throbbing dick.

The women got on the pallet on their hands and knees just like he'd told them, though he had to gently push on both of their backs so that they put their chests down on the cardboard. He lifted their dresses up over their hips, then dove inside of Linda's pussy first, while fingering Cheryl.

"Ooooh! Mmmm! Fuck yes!" Linda screamed, as she immediately started cumming all over Tony's thrusting member. Cheryl rubbed her friends back, then kissed her, letting Linda moan into her mouth.

"Oh, yeah! This some good white pussy. Mmmm," Tony moaned, then put his left thumb in his mouth, got it nice and wet, and then stuck it in Cheryl's ass.

"Awwww! Yes, work it in there," Cheryl cried.

Tony pulled out of Linda's pussy and dove right into Cheryl's asshole, his dick lubricated with Linda's cream.

"Oh, fuck! Oh, GOD damn!" Tony moaned, pumping away. He reached over and played with Linda's clit as he continued to slam into Cheryl's ass. He was going to bust any second now.

"Awww, shit! Where y'all want it at? Hungh?" he said, as his thrusts got shorter and quicker.

"Cum...cuming...cum in my ass!" Cheryl screamed.

"I want some in my pussy," Linda said, playing with her clit.

Tony gave two or three more good pumps and then he exploded into Cheryl's asshole. He reached down after two good squirts and gripped his dick tightly, the pressure to release mounting.

He then slid his dick all the way into Linda's pussy and let go of his load, blasting the last squirts of cum deep inside Linda's thirsty womb.

After he finished his eruption a voice came over the speakers system of the grocery store: **"Clean up on aisle five! Clean up on aisle five!**

VIP

~~~~~~

"So ok, let me get this straight. You expect me to have a threesome with you and another girl whenever you want, but you wouldn't want to have a threesome with me and another guy!?" Mellisa said with a smirk on her face to her boyfriend Zach, after they'd just finished a sweaty fuck session with her friend Amy and were now out on his balcony sharing a cigarette.

"Mellisa, I hope you know you sound like a fucking nympho slash whore when you talk like that. I mean, being with two women at the same time allows us both pleasure at the same time, but two men in the same bed doesn't equal pleasure to me, and sounds kinda gay to be honest," Zach replied in a matter of fact tone..

"Gay!? Ha! You're such a pig it's ridiculous! It's always about you, Zach, never me. And that's not fair! Plus, we agreed from the beginning that what's good for one is certainly good for the other. Remember that?" Mellisa exclaimed.

"So what am I supposed to do, huh? Walk up to some stranger in a bar or club and ask him to come and help me bone my girl down for the evening!?" he replied, getting frustrated with where the conversation had went.

"Well, actually I have someone in mind, if it's ok with you," Mellisa replied.

"Really? Really? Well, who the hell is he for crying out loud already!" Zach said, now feeling his manhood being tested.

Sure, he could suggest what friends of hers that would be great for their threesomes, but this new idea she was talking about was testing his limits.

"His name's Darius, but everybody calls him Big D. He was dating my old friend Nicky a while ago, but she broke it off after she saw some of the home made videos he's got floating around with some of his ex's," she said.

"And just how in the hell did you meet this Darius guy?!" Zach yelled, shocked at his girlfriend's admission, and for being interested in being fucked by another man. Zach was becoming more and more jealous as she talked.

"Well, I saw a few of the home made videos he's in one weekend when me and a bunch of the girls went to the Lake of the Ozarks. And then when we all came back in town, we'd went to the Power and Light District and I met him in person because he was a bouncer at a club we couldn't get into, but he was cool enough to let us in when the club wasn't letting anyone else in for the night. He'd gave us his card and told us that if we ever wanted to come back to call him ahead of time and he'd make sure we got in," she said.

"So what are you saying? You're just gonna call him up and say, come over to my place and I'd like for you and my boyfriend to fuck me at the same time!?" Zach said sarcastically.

"No, dummie. I'd call him and tell him that we're coming to the club and the two of you would meet there. If you decide he's cool, then we'll make the decision then. I'm telling you Zach, he's really nice and laid-back so it won't be awkward at all. He's one of those brothers that everybody likes," Mellisa replied, ignoring his sarcasm.

"Wait a fucking minute. HE'S BLACK!!?? WHAT THE FUCK MELLISA!!?? YOU ACTUALLY EXPECT ME TO SHARE MY GIRL WITH SOME BIG DICK BROTHER!!?? ARE YOU OUTTA YOUR FUCKING MIND!!??" Zach yelled loudly on the balcony, turning a bright red.

"Oh, would you please calm down before you wake up everybody in the damn neighborhood, for Christ sake! As a matter of fact, since you're all intimidated by him being a brother and all, forget I even mentioned it, Zach," she said, dismissing their conversation.

"ME intimidated!?! HA! Don't make me laugh, Mellisa! I'll show you and Darius or whoever he is that I'm not intimidated by any other man on this earth! So if you wanna a DP session, then that's exactly what your ass shall have! Call him and set it up. Game on!" Zach exclaimed, trying to save face.

Mellisa was thrilled and couldn't wait to have her threesome with Darius the Big D. She'd heard the rumors, and saw the video tapes, witnessing first hand his monster cock in action. Once she'd met him personally, she knew she had to find a way to get some of that big cock she'd been fantasizing about in her dreams.

The club speakers blasted a deep bass that felt as if the floor was vibrating, and the different colors in lighting made it seem as though they'd came into another world as Mellisa and Zach entered Club S.O.A.K. in the Power and Light District.

Mellisa had called Darius to make sure they wouldn't have any trouble getting in, and as he'd promised they were given access, topped with a V.I.P. pass that gave them a secluded booth that had a privacy curtain and a bottle on the house.

Darius promised them that before the night was over he'd come up to V.I.P. to check on his guest.

"So what do you think so far Zach!?" Mellisa shouted over the loud crowd, as they moved through the sea of people tightly packed into the club.

"This place is live! I can see now why you'd almost have to know someone to get in here!
It's off the chain for real!" he replied smiling, and pulling her into him and kissing her neck.

Zach had done a quick head count when he'd first came in and immediately noticed that there were more women inside than men. This was definitely his type of atmosphere, he'd thought to himself.

His initial feeling after seeing and meeting Darius for the first time at the entrance was that he actually did seem very cool and approachable, which exclaimed why he'd been standing in a circle of hot chicks when he and Mellisa had arrived. Darius was taller than Zach and more muscular as well, but Zach wrote that off quickly, saying to himself that that was only because of Darius' employment, having to stay in shape and all, but this guy wasn't nearly as intimidating as he'd imagined.

"I'm glad you like it, honey! Now let's get up to V.I.P. and pop some bottles!" Mellisa shouted with her hands in the air.

Mellisa and Zach mingled with the V.I.P. crowd, sipping champagne and downing shots of Ciroc with the groups of partiers. Once the two had made their way back to their booth, Zach closed the privacy curtain and was all over Mellisa.

He kissed her passionately up and down her neck, nibbling at her earlobes while his hands raced all over her body.

Mellisa was turned on immediately, moaning and breathing heavily as she stroked his hardening cock through his slacks.

"I want you so bad right now," he breathed into her ear.

"I want you to take me right here in this booth, Zach. I'm so wet right now," she panted, sliding closer into him.

Zach slid his hands up her sheer dress, to her inner thighs, feeling the warmth coming from her honey pot instantly. He pulled the front of her panties to the side and slid his middle finger into her wetness slowly. He stroked her hot slit, and pulled his fingers from her to taste her juices.

"AHH Zach! I want it inside of me so bad right now. Baby, take your dick out now," she begged, as he continued to kiss her neck and went back to fingering her tight hole.

Zach did as she requested and unzipped his slacks, and adjusted his boxers so that his hardness was set free..

Mellisa quickly straddled him in the booth, sinking herself onto his hard cock in one swift motion. She tongued him wildly while gripping a handful of his hair.

"AHH! Fuck! Your cock feels so good, baby! Grab my ass, Zach. Yea, yea, that's it! Squeeze my ass! While I cum," she moaned, grinding down into him, bucking her hips.

Darius had been standing and watching Mellisa and Zach through the curtain. Mellisa had told him just how she wanted him to make his entrance for the evening. She wanted to taste his black meat first, before being thoroughly fucked and she came all over it.

"Well, the two of you don't seem to need any help from me to get the party started," Darius said as he stepped inside closing the curtain tightly behind himself.

Zach looked up quickly to notice Darius making his way towards them.

"Bring that big cock over here so I can suck it while I ride my man Zach's at the same time," Mellisa commanded with a smile.

Darius approached the booth from the backside. His erection had grown from previously watching the two, and now he pulled his hardening member from his pants, headed for Mellisa's watering mouth.

Zach initially froze, but once he saw how nonchalant and relaxed Darius was and how Mellisa was really turned on, he decided to go along with the flow and not show any signs of insecurity.

"Yea, let me see you suck his cock Mellisa! And you better suck it good. Yea, show him what I taught you," Zach said, still thrusting upward into her snatch.

"Oh, my God! Look at that beautiful cock!" Mellisa said as she held Darius in her hands before taking the tip of his eleven inches into her mouth, licking his sticky precum.

Out of the corner of Zach's eye, he could see the biggest cock he'd ever witnessed and his girlfriend was sucking and nursing the tip like an ice cold popsicle on a hot summer day.

Mellisa stared Darius in his eyes while attempting to deep throat him all at once.

"Don't be greedy, baby girl. Just take your time and use your tongue," Darius coached her as he held her head in place with her ponytail.

"Honey, I wanna suck your cock now. Switch places with Darius. I want him to feel this tight and hot pussy, and I want to taste my juices on your cock," Mellisa said huskily into Zach's ear, while dismounting his manhood with ease. She was ready to be filled with what she came for.

Darius hopped over the booth in one swift leap and took the seat in the booth while Zach stood up. Mellisa stood, placing both feet on either side of Darius' legs, and slowly sank onto his rock solid cock, taking as much of him into her as she could initially withstand.

"Fuck your cock is huge! And it feels so good to my pussy!" she moaned, wrapping her arms around his shoulders, breathing heavily while getting warmed up to his presence within her walls.

Darius reached behind her, palming and squeezing her firm backside.

"Is this what you like, huh? Tell me if this is what you like, Mellisa," Darius said into her ear.

"YES! YES! THIS IS WHAT I LIKE! SMACK MY ASS DARIUS!" She quickly exclaimed, bucking wildly in his lap.

Darius pumped her tight cunt hard and fast from below, meeting her thrust and filled her completely with all eleven inches of himself. Mellisa's inner walls began to contract and her body stiffened.

"HOLY FUCK! OH SHIT! HOLY FUCK! I'M GONNA CUM ALL OVER YOUR COCK! OH FUCK DARIUS, I'M CUMMING ALL OVER YOUR BIG BLACK DICK."

Mellisa screamed and an orgasm ripped thru her body like a tidal wave. Darius continued to stroke her hot slit from below as she relaxed her head on his shoulder..

"Oh no you don't, sweetheart! The party's just getting started!" Zach said while moving in and grabbing her by her ponytail, and shoving his sticky five-inches into her mouth. "NOW SUCK IT!" he continued.

Mellisa loved being aggressed sexually, and this fueled her fire. She took Zach into her mouth and sucked him aggressively, knowing how he loved to be deep throated.

"Let me stand her up," Darius said, sliding from underneath Mellisa, now positioning her on her knees with him behind her as she went to work on Zach, who was fucking Mellisa's mouth with haste.

"I'm gonna take you from behind now, Mellisa. This way I can really spank your ass good, and I know you're gonna like it," Darius said, spreading her open from behind.

Mellisa reached back with both hands and helped him hold her open, fully exposing her dripping cunt to him now. Darius entered her hot and wet slit hard and fast, sinking himself into her balls deep.

"OOHHH!!! OOHHH MY FUCKING GODDDDDDD!!!!! YEA! FUCK ME!!!! YEAH FUCK ME HARD JUST LIKE THAT!!!" shescreamed as Darius pounded her hard, deep, and fast, giving her ass a royal spanking at the same time.

"Give it all to me, Mellisa! Yea! Yea! That's right! Fuck me back! Yea, throw that ass back at me while I'm fucking you!" Darius continued.

Mellisa felt Zach expand in her mouth and as his grip tightened on the back of her head, she tasted his explosion of hot cum into her mouth.

"AAUUHHHH!!! FUCK your mouth is so fucking good, baby! You're a natural cocksucker, baby!" Zach shouted as he spilled the remainder of his load into her mouth.

One down, one to go, she smiled to herself.

"Stick your fingers in my ass, Darius! I want your fingers in my ass, right now! I'm gonna cum all over that big dick again!" she said, going wild and thrusting back into him.

Zach looked on in amazement as she took every inch of Darius without hesitation. Darius spit on his two thumbs, grabbed and spread her ass cheeks firmly, and plunged them into her forbidden flower, locking her into position while speeding up the pace of his stroke.

"UMM! AUAHH! That's it baby! Take this big dick, baby!!" Darius shouted as he relentlessly pounded her tight pussy from behind.

"OOO I'M GONNA CUM AGAINI! OEEWWWW! Fuck me harder! Harder! AWWWWW!" she cried out in passion as she gushed out another climax.. Her climax had brought Darius to the boiling point, and his load needed to be spilled so he pulled out of her quickly.

"Turn around and come and get this!" he groaned huskily.

Mellisa dove for his cock, grabbing him with both hands and milking every drop of the thick and rich cream into her wanting mouth.

"AUUHHHH!!!!! GERRRRR!!!!" Darius grunted as his knees suddenly felt weak from his release.

"I knew there was something special about you the first time I met you, Mellisa," he said smiling down at her.

As the three left the V.I.P. section, Darius gave them two passes that they could use whenever they revisited the club.

"As much as I appreciate the two of y'alls company, I gotta report to management before they wonder where I've been. But please come back to see me anytime, though the pleasure's been all mine," Darius said with a smile, giving Mellisa a light hug, and Zach a firm handshake before disappearing into a crowd of people.

"Thank you, honey," Mellisa whispered in Zach's ear and kissed him on the cheek as they exited Club Soak.

"Thank me for what, baby?" Zach asked puzzled.

"For letting your D.A.W.G. off the leash tonight," she smiled as the valet pulled their car up for them.

———

A Penny Publication
dawgtailsinfo@gmail.com
https://www.amazon.com/author/dawgtales